Crash
THE IMMORTAL CHRONICLES

BY

SLOANE MURPHY

Crash
The Immortal Chronicles #2
Copyright © 2017 by Sloane Murphy
www.authorsloanemurphy.com

Cover Design by Steam Power Studios | Edited by Katie John
| Formatted by Sloane Murphy

Soar/Sloane Murphy – 2nd ed.
ISBN-13 - 9781723774683

Dedication

To everyone who ever took a chance on love.

For those who sacrificed everything, even themselves, to feel the greatest of feelings.

This is for you.

All the Gods, all the Heavens,
all the Hells, are within you.

~ Joseph Campbell

 Chapter One

XANDER

Ten years ago

"Dimitri my friend, I have a new task for you," I say. I can feel his weariness; he hates it when I do this to him, but he always takes it in his stride. He's my most loyal friend, and my most trusted advisor.

He hesitates. "I don't like the sound of that. What do you need from me?" he asks.

"I need you to take the open teaching position at the Academy."

"Are you kidding me? You want me to look after those monsters? I'd rather deal with a horde of Demons than snotty kids."

"'fraid not friend. I can't explain it right now, but I need you to do this for me."

1

"Did I do something to piss you off?" he asks, letting out a puff of laughter.

"The total opposite, my friend! I need someone I trust. You are my best fighter, and my most loyal friend, which is why I need you to do this for me."

He narrows his eyes and rubs at his chin. He is analysing me. "Hmm, there's something you're not telling me."

"There is, but I just need you to trust me for now."

"Okay. Why the hell not? I could use a change of pace I suppose. Ali and Selina have made it their mission lately to torture me. At least this will be a whole new type of torture," he says and I laugh. He has never let me down. Not once.

"Thank you D. This means more to me than you know."

"No worries. When do I start?" he asks.

I reach up and scratch the back of my neck. "We, er… we head to the academy tonight. You start tomorrow with the new inductees from the nurseries. They're due in in the morning."

"Nothing like being confident in getting what you want," he laughs, patting me on the back. "I guess I better go and pack up my stuff. How long is this for?" he asks.

"For now, I don't know, but it's probably not a short-term thing."

"Indefinitely. Awesome, got it. Loving all the information you've got for me, man."

One year later

"She's the reason you asked me to take this job, isn't she?" Dimitri asks as we watch Addie play in the field with her friends.

"She is," I confess.

"I don't know how I knew, but I just did. She's spectacular. Even at this age, she shows more promise in this class than almost any other person I've ever trained. Why her?"

"Her parents died, but before they did, they asked me to keep her safe. I swore I would; I've watched out for her since she was born."

"You managed to do that along with everything else, and with none of us knowing? Dude, you're like superman. I have no idea how you did it. I barely manage to remember all of the little monsters' names!" he laughs.

"It wasn't too big a problem; I just made sure she had everything she needed. Money, clothes – the necessities. The Keepers did the majority of the hard work, and they gave me monthly reports on her progress throughout nursery. But the Academy is different. Her time here is important, so I made sure I was Head of the Board. And, when I heard about the open space for defence, I knew I needed you to fill it. Her life probably isn't going to be easy; she's going to need a teacher she can trust. A friend," I tell him.

He slips me a questioning look. I can tell he's dying to ask me more, but I know he won't.

"She seems happy," I continue. "And she has friends. Not many, mind you, but I think that's her choice. She's not exactly open to new people. Those four," I say, nodding my head in her direction where she is playing with her friends, "stick together like bloody glue. They're almost inseparable. Especially the girls." I pause for a moment, enjoying the sound of their laughter in the sunlight. "However," I muse, "Tyler seems a little off to me, especially when he's on his own. I've observed him and his behaviour is… well it's obscure."

"They were raised together in nursery and formed a tight bond – like family," I explain to Dimitri, "Especially after Olivia's parents died. You'd be amazed at the strings I had to pull to ensure they stayed together here. The boys though." I tut and shake my head. "I was not so happy about those, especially Tyler. He has a report list longer than my arm from times he was in trouble, instigated or not. But I had to pick between Addie and Olivia staying together or which room she got. I felt it was more important that she stay with Olivia. I just hope their friendship with the boys doesn't last long" I sigh.

4

"Anyone would think you were jealous, friend." Dimitri laughs. "After all, for Immortals, age is pretty irrelevant."

"Don't be ridiculous, Dimitri. She is my ward. I care for her as anyone else in my position would."

"Never say never, Xander. Anything can happen. Forever is a long time."

CRASH

Chapter Two

ADDIE

Present Day

I lift my head and wake to my new hell – yet again. Each time I pass out, I wake hoping it's all a nightmare. The light above me flickers and the harshness of it burns my eyes causing me to squint through swollen flesh to see if I'm alone. I am. That's one small relief. The dripping of water from the leaking pipes above me is another torture all of its own.

I try to stretch, but the restraints holding me in the chair make it almost impossible. The sores on my wrists and ankles crack open as I move them again, my skin tearing from where it's knitted to the leather straps during my sleep. Fresh blood surfaces. I refuse to give in; they will not break me. I have no idea what they want from me, but I won't let them win.

7

Exhaustion washes over me. I've been here since Cole made his announcement that he's my father. I'm still not sure how I feel about it, or even if I should believe it. I have no idea what he would gain from lying to me about it, and he's done nothing yet to prove I can trust one word that comes out of his mouth. Since my arrival here, I've been almost constantly in this wretched chair – and I've not seen Cole again. Not that I really expect to. If he *is* my father, he's proven before that he is good at leaving. My time here has been spent being tortured. I've been punched, stabbed, slashed, and electrocuted by the Demons keeping me here. I've lost track of time; there are no windows, no way of telling if it's night or day. I've done nothing but fight to stay alive. To stay me.

Desperation claws at my thoughts. *Will I survive them next time? Will I ever get out of here?* I hear footsteps coming down the hall and try to squash the feeling of fear that rises from my stomach. Even if I'm dying inside, I'll be damned if I let them see it. Then I hear Micah's' laugh; that same sadistic laugh I've heard almost every day as he tears or burns my skin. The sound makes me sick to my stomach. Each time I hear it, my hope plummets further into the abyss.

"Ooohhhhh, Addie. Wakey, wakey, Princess! It's a special, special day!" His nasal voice is like nails on a chalkboard. He rounds the corner and claps his grubby hands together giddily. The sight of him makes my heart

8

flip. He might look like a slimy, creepy human but this douche is all demon.

"Oh, Princess, why don't you look happy to see me? I thought we were friends. I don't like it when people aren't my friend." His face transforms from ecstatically happy to utter rage within seconds; the craziness however, never leaves his eyes. He opens the door to my holding cell, laughing to himself as he disables the electric charge, which runs through the metal. He's tall and slim – lanky almost. The bright electric lights highlight the grease that slicks his green hair from his face.

"Not even a good morning Addie? How rude! Princesses really should have better manners. No worry – once we're done with you, you'll be the perfect princess, won't you? Yes, you will," he says the last part of that sentence more for his own benefit than for mine. He locks the door behind him and a new surge of fear washes over me. He looks at me, taking in my wretched state. His sneer makes my blood run cold. "Todays a special day Princess," he says. "We have guests joining us. Isn't that good news?" He works his way around the room, and I lose sight of him as he goes to the table behind me. The scrape of metal on metal makes me shudder. *Not again*, I pray.

He comes back in front of me again, dishevelled, as if he hasn't bothered to change or shower in weeks. It's his demented smile that creeps me out the most. He actually enjoys the daily hell he puts me through. He's Coles lapdog, just one of many I think, but he gets the pleasure of being my host. Micah treats Cole as if the sun shines out of his ass. He's loyal to a fault and a generally all-round dickhead.

"Why? Why are you doing this?" I ask. I ask this question almost every day, but I rarely get a response.

"Oh, Princess, you know why we're doing this. You have so much potential. You have no idea just how much power you hold. I'm doing all of this to help you; to help you unlock that potential so you can be all that you can be," he says with his resident sadistic chuckle. He edges closer to me, knife in hand. "Are you ready yet, princess? Ready to be a better version of yourself?" I can't bite back my scream. Pain rips through every inch of me as the metal scores across my chest and is mixed with the electrical current he sends through me. As he sends another shot of electricity into me, my head shoots back, smashing on the back of the chair, the pain is minimal compared to the shocks. I unequivocally despise Demons, but I especially hate this god damned Kaiji!

He claps his hands gleefully – the crazy, sadistic weirdo.

"You're so close to the edge, Princess. I can feel the power in you trying to break free."

I try to catch my breath. I barely have the strength to lift my head.

"What makes you think it'll ever be free?" I wheeze. I'm so angry and so weak that the rage is channelling through me. I swallow down the pain of another deep intake of breath. I have things I want to say to the bastard. I am defiant, despite everything. "And even if it does surface," I say, using all my remaining strength to lift my head and meet his eyes, "You, Micah, will be the first person I hunt down and kill." I spit the words out, each one potent with the rage I feel inside

"Oooooo scary," he mocks. "Once your power is unleashed, you'll thank me. The boss will be so happy." He moves closer to me and wraps his hands around my throat, pinning me to the chair.

"Our company is here now, Princess; it's time for the real fun to begin," he whispers in my ear, licking my cheek before he moves away from me. Every part of me wants to break down and cry. I feel so violated, but I can't let them see they're winning.

I can feel the power coming before I see anyone. My newest senses are overloaded from the strength heading in my direction. The pressure builds inside my skull as they get closer. I'm too weak to put up any sort of wall to keep them out. Then I see them. Seven women, or rather Demons. Each is putting out a different power – a sign that each is a different type of demon.

I recall being taught about the fearless Seven. They are Cole's version of an Elite. Each one is as ruthless and deadly as the next; cold blooded assassins with no conscience. Not that you'd know that to look at them, which I guess is what makes them so good at what they do. The Seven are feared throughout my world, and a lot of people believe that Cole would never have got as far as he did in the Dark War if it wasn't for them. The Seven are known to lead The Hordes of Hell, the Demons who live in the shadows, and for some reason, they decided to follow Cole.

"Goodie! You're here!" Micah squeals before bowing down to them.

What the hell? I think. He is completely unhinged. He unlocks the door and in single file they filter in. "Lieutenants," Micah says acting as Master of Ceremonies, "I'd like you to meet Adelaide Tate, my latest project. She's been so much fun to play with," he says, casting a look in my direction before lowering his voice to entertain himself, "Way more than the last one."

I watch as The Seven appraise me like a piece of livestock.

"It certainly looks like you've been having fun, Micah," says the demon in the red dress.

Micah brushes aside her undercurrent of criticism and his eyes fall on me. "Addie, these are Cole's Lieutenants." He points to them each as he names them and my eyes track them, taking in their variants. Suki, the demon at the front looks Asian. She is beautiful, with long sleek black

12

hair. Her dress, which trails the floor, is made of red silk; a slit at the side exposes her lean thigh. She looks more ready for a party than a day at the office. I will never understand Demons. The others are just as beautiful. Ivy is pale as snow with shoulder length raven hair and piercing blue eyes, she looks harmless, almost waife-like, but the look in her eyes makes my blood run cold.

Ruby has olive skin, with hair as dark as night and eyes to match, she's decked out in leather from head to toe, and looks kind of badass.

Rue has dark skin and red eyes, with long red hair, and on closer inspection, her skin looks like scales. *Gross.*

Salem and Prosperine are twins. They look like something out of the notebook; both fair, with blue eyes and golden hair. Salem's falls in big curls down her back, whereas Prosperine's is dead straight. Her smile throws me for a moment – it almost seems kind and genuine, but I'm not going to count on that.

Luce looks like she just stepped off of a runway. Her dark hair is cut in a harsh straight bob at her chin with thick bangs, framing her small face, but it's her purple eyes that shock me, I thought only Fae had those!

"We're here to get an update for the boss, Micah," Suki declares. "Has there been any progress?"

"Of course, Suki. My apologies. I can Demonstrate if you like?" he replies.

13

"Please, if you would." She nods at him before crossing her arms and turning her attention to me. She is fearsome. I wouldn't fancy my chances against her in a fight – she has that kind of way about her that suggests she'd laugh as she ripped your head off.

"Nothing like asking first, and you say I have no manners. Who exactly are these ass clowns you're bowing down to? Anyone fancy letting me in on any sort of information?" I mutter, the sarcasm thick but no-one is paying any attention to what I'm saying.

"You'll be able to feel the spike in her power," Micah explains. "Pay attention to her eyes. Aeveen is fighting to break through." He walks towards me and places his palms on my forearms, looking me in the eyes. "Time to play," he says with a cruel glint in his eyes.

The current rips through me again, stronger than any I've felt before. My scream echoes around the room and I feel myself detach; I can't feel the pain anymore because I'm watching on from the outside.

"Let me out, Addie. I'll make it all stop. I will kill him and anyone else who dares to try and hurt us."

I hear the voice in my head trying to work out where it came from. I think I've finally lost it.

"I'm here to help you, Addie. All you have to do is give in and let me out. Just for a minute."

What the hell! I start to panic, and that's when I feel it – the power building up inside me, fighting me, wanting to break free. I try to hold it, but there's just too much. I slip away from my body and watch as the pain fades from my face and *she* takes over.

An evil smile has spread across my jaw. *Holy crow, my eyes!* They're glowing red as, the bindings undo around my wrists and my hands wrap around Micah's throat stopping his screams. I watch on in horror at the things my body is doing without my control over it. My nails extend into claws and pierce his skin. I do not flinch as his blood runs over my hands.

"You will pay for what you have done to us, Micah Andrews." The voice that comes from my body is not mine; it's raspy and seductive, as if she's actually getting off on his pain. Smoke starts to rise from his skin. Within moments, flames wrap around him, but in spite of the fierce heat, I'm still holding on to him. I smile as he burns.

"Enough!" Suki shouts. She raises her hand, sending Micah flying out of my grasp and across the room. She turns to me and I see the uncertainty on her face. She masks it quickly, taking a step towards me, a flick of her hands retying the straps holding me to the chair. Her eyes narrow. "Who are you?" she asks.

"My name is Aeveen, but you already knew that, Suki the Djinn." My head tilts as we study her. "You are afraid, Suki. I can feel your fear."

"Wait, how do you know who she is?" I ask. I have no idea what the hell is going on. Am I losing my mind finally? Did they win?

"Hush Adelaide, I know many things. I will explain in time."

"I am not afraid of you, Great One. Who do you answer to? Where do your allegiances fall?"

My mouth is moving but I'm not thinking – Aeveen is doing that for us. "I follow no-one, my allegiance is to myself, and definitely not to those who have tortured us."

"We have done nothing that wasn't necessary to allow you to be free," Suki says forcefully.

I think I've finally lost my mind. I feel a pull and things go blurry for a few seconds. I blink my eyes to clear my vision and open them to find I'm me again. I look around the room frantically, but I'm alone. *What the fuck was that?*

Footsteps travel down the dirt corridor. I'm still stuck in this goddamn chair, and I'm horrifically disgusting. They've kept me in this chair for weeks, only letting me leave to go relieve myself in a bucket in the corner.

"Addie?" I know that voice but in the darkness, it's hard to trace its location. I sit up and search the shadows.

"Logan?" I ask, almost not daring to hope. I've hallucinated plenty of times. It feels like forever since I last saw him. For a long time, I thought he was dead; that I'd never see those cute little dimples of his again.

"Yeah, it's me, Addie. Are you okay?" I can't help but laugh as the memory of Kaden singing to me pops into my head. So inappropriate.

"Addie?"

"Oh yeah, I'm walking on fucking rainbows and shitting unicorns. Does it look like I'm okay?" He winces under the lash of my tongue. "Sorry," I say quietly. "I didn't mean to bite your head off. How are you even here?"

"It's okay, Ads… honestly, from you, I expected worse." His small smile brings back so many memories from forever ago. "I've been trying so hard to get down here to you since you got here. He wouldn't let me, and since I'm so new, there's nothing I could do," he pleads. I want to feel bad for him but I can't. "I am so sorry, Addie. What they've done to you – I tried to stop it, I really did. But I'm nothing here."

"It's okay, you're here now. Can you help me?" I ask. I can't remember ever having felt so desperate.

A look of guilt spreads across his face, and my hope fades. "If I could, I would, Addie. You know that."

"So why are you even here?" I bite, the venom thick in my voice.

17

"I... I wanted to check in on you: to make sure you were okay – and yes, I know that's stupid, but I wanted to see my friend."

"My friend would help me get out of here, Logan."

"I'm sorry, Addie. I would if I could."

"Just go," I say. The anger burns through me.

His shoulders droop.

"I really am sorry, Addie," he says quietly before walking away and taking the sliver of what little hope I had with him.

"Where are we?" I ask, looking around at the beauty surrounding me. I don't know that I've ever been anywhere so calming, so serene. I look out over the view in front of me. When we broke through the trees, I was met by the sight of grass and rocks; a small pool being fed by a waterfall.

"Xander, this place is beautiful!" I say twirling around before running and jumping into his arms causing him to drop the basket he's been carrying. I pepper his face with chaste kisses. He twirls me in circles before lowering me back to the ground, then gathers my face in his hands and kisses me. The kisses are different this time – deeper but still gentle.

"It's nothing compared to you, but I thought you might like it. I came across it whilst I was on my last scout. I saw it and thought of you," he says, resting his forehead on mine. His lips are so close they tease me. Each moment, I crave them more. The butterflies in my stomach take flight and I close my eyes to hide the emotion I know he'll see there.

"Don't hide from me, Addie. You never have to hide – not from me," he says, gripping my chin. I don't think I've ever been happier than in this moment.

"You make me feel again," he says. "It's been a long time since I could say that. Even if nobody else knows, I always want you to know that I love you. I will love you until my lungs give out; until there is nothing more than dust on this earth, and long after that still. I will never feel love again like I love you."

Tears prick at the corners of my eyes. I don't know what I did to deserve him, but I'm thankful for him coming into my life each and every day. He pulls me into his chest and hugs me so tightly that I can't tell where I end and he begins. I close my eyes and sink into him, bunching my hands in his sweater and holding on tight. I want to remember this moment forever.

"I love you too, Xander; more than I ever thought possible." He kisses me gently before walking me backwards towards the small rock pool. He shakes from my grasp and I watch, full of giggles, as he pulls out a

19

blanket from the basket he brought with him. Proud of his endeavours, he sits down and pats the ground beside him. As I go to join him, he pulls me into his arms and we fall backwards, my head landing on his chest. I've never felt so content with silence before, but he just makes it so easy. Being with him makes everything else fade away.

The day passes by as we talk about his past; he tells me about his childhood, about the chaos he and Kaden used to cause. I could tell he was keeping something from me, but I didn't want to pry and ruin our day. I look up at the now dark sky, the stars seem so bright tonight.

"Doesn't it make you feel so small? They're so far away, and they last so long. It makes me remember I'm part of something bigger," he says wistfully.

"I've never really thought about it. I think they're pretty, but I don't know much about astrology," I admit.

"That surprises me, some of the most beautiful stories are told in the stars," he says, pointing up to the brightest star in the sky. "That there is Vega. My father told me Vega was a celestial princess who fell in love with a mortal, Kengyu. That's his star over there. Her Father, the King, found out about their great love and it angered him greatly that she could love someone so far beneath her. In his rage, he forbade her to ever see him again. They were parted forever, even in death because of the King's wishes. The two lovers were placed in the sky, where they were separated by the Celestial River, known to us as

Milky Way. Yet the sky Gods are kind. Each year, on the seventh night of the seventh moon, a bridge of magpie's forms across the Celestial River, and the two lovers are reunited. My Father always told me that true love can never be stopped: it will last beyond the ages. I saw that kind of love in his eyes when he looked at my mother. When she smiled, he looked like he could walk the moon."

"Xander, that is so beautiful! I wish we could stay here forever."

I stir from my dream, but for a second I deny reality, and I stay there with him. I feel so at peace, I don't want to open my eyes and ruin it. I want to stay there forever, but as reality crashes down on me piece by piece, drawing me back into what my life has become, I fight to keep the tears at bay.

I can hear Micah's snigger as he prances towards my cell. His crazy, sadistic nature makes every hair on my body stand up, but I can't escape. This awful chair is my newest hell.

"Hello, Princess. Ready for another day with me? I bet you can't wait," he says with the biggest of smiles. "I so look forward to our time together! I cherish it. It's my favourite time of day!" He walks towards me, and it's as if he's so excited he's almost shaking.

21

"Fuck you, Micah! You and your savage, psychotic ways. As soon as I get free from here, I'll finish what we started yesterday," I say to him quietly.

"Now, now princess, what's with all this hostility? I just want to be friends. Help you be the best you can be," he says with a perverse giggle. "Plus, we have more guests today, so you need to be on your best behaviour!" He walks behind me, heading back to the table that is home to his torture equipment. I hear the sound of metal on metal, accompanied by that annoying as hell giggle of his. He jumps in front of me with a flourish as if this all a big show.

"Time for you to sleep Princess! Can't have you being bad in front of our guests again."

LIVVY

"Syre, you asked for me?" I say, stepping into his office. I officially hate this room, this place, and sometimes, this man, but I can do nothing but submit and survive. He's sat there behind that massive mahogany desk, his chin resting on his steepled fingers as if he's the most important man in the world. His arrogance kills me. Why are the pretty ones always asshats?

"Ah, Olivia, yes, come in. I wanted to thank you for doing so well on your little recon mission and bringing Adelaide to me so quickly and efficiently. The way you planned so precisely and carried out the task was spectacular. I am very pleased with your progress here."

"Thank you, Syre," I say, bowing my head.

"I need you to help me with her, Olivia. I need you to befriend her again. Get close to her. I need her to trust you. Without that, our whole plan will fail. We need her to believe us when we tell her she's a demon, Olivia. She cannot know that we're lying to her," he says to me.

Well. Bend me over and take me on a Tuesday. How the hell am I meant to do that?

"I will try my best, Syre, although considering everything, I may not be the best person for the job. I've already betrayed her once. Plus, Addie has always been so self-righteous. I'm not sure how easy it will be to convince her."

"That's what's so perfect about it. You can feed on her emotions, about how you're stuck here too. How we made you do it. I know you're a manipulative little bitch, that's how you've managed to climb my ranks so quickly. Do not disappoint me, Olivia. Between you and Micah, I expect her to believe everything we tell her. She will be broken. Do you understand me?"

"Of course, Syre. I'll think of something. Do I have permission to take her out of her cell?"

"Anything you need to do. You're dismissed," he says before shooing me out of his office.

23

Egotistical asshole. I leave the room, closing the door behind me. *How the hell am I meant to do this?* There is no way in Hell she's going to trust me again. Not that I blame her, I'd be the same if our roles were reversed.

I can't believe how much of a whiney little bitch she's become. I'm the one that was tortured, the one turned into this monster, not her. Boo-fucking-hoo for her. She got the guy, and from what I've heard, she replaced me, too. Even Kaden ended up batting for her against Cole. I've never seen anyone go against Cole before. That day was horrific. Kaden, Michael, and Celeste stormed in here, wings out, full defensive.

They walked through the foyer and straight to the back of the house where Cole was training with me and a few other new recruits. At the time, they were friends, we thought we had nothing to fear from them, how wrong we were. The other recruits and I were dismissed into the house by Cole before the fighting began. When it happened, nobody had any idea what was going on. Then we found out the truth. We had been betrayed by Kaden, he had turned against us. He became the enemy in that moment. After that was when Cole came to me with my mission. Another way for me to seal my fate here. A way to earn his favour. I jumped at the chance, a chance to work closer with him, to be closer to him.

Betraying Addie wasn't an issue. She's no one to me anymore. I have a new family now.

ADDIE

"Adelaide, wake up." I stir and realise I'm in a new room. Well, new cell, a room would be too generous of a description for where I am. Much to my relief, I realize I'm not in that chair anymore! I'm lying down on what is possibly the lumpiest, hardest excuse for a bed I've ever been on but compared to the chair it's absolute heaven! The walls and floor in here are still filthy, and another leaking pipe. *Joys. Does nothing work properly down here?* The fluorescent light above me is bright, and flickers.

Slowly, I sit up. I've barely eaten since I've been here and finally being able to move makes me realize how weak I feel.

"Adelaide!" I hear the impatient voice again and understand it wasn't a figment of my imagination. I've hallucinated a lot since I've been here, my grasp on reality slips further each day. I look towards where the voice came from and see more bars making up the fourth wall of the room. Sat outside is Cole.

"Good, you're up."

"Not like you gave me much choice, is it?" I snarl. I really don't like being caged.

"Now then, Adelaide – that's no way to speak to your father. I came down here to speak to my daughter, but if you're going to act like nothing more than a feral animal, I won't bother," he says, sighing in disappointment.

Asshole. He doesn't get to be disappointed. He abandoned me, then changed his mind and put me through hell before locking me in this grimy hellhole of a prison. He can do one. I roll my eyes at him before sitting up.

"Oh, I'm terribly sorry, daddy dearest. Should I give you my fullest attention? You'll understand if after everything, I'm not exactly inclined to give a shit!"

"Adelaide, if you'd listen to me, you would realize I don't want to keep you here like this, but we need to build some semblance of trust before I let you out of there. I need to know that you're open to listening to me. Hearing my side as it were."

"You expect me to trust you? After everything? You basically killed two of my best friends, turned the other one against me, then locked me in this hell hole. All of this after abandoning me in the first place. Super effort there."

"I can tell you're not in any shape to have an adult conversation," he says sighing heavily.

I really couldn't give less of a shit how disappointed he is.

"You'll come around to my way of thinking," he says. "One way or another, Adelaide; you'll see."

"Prepare yourself for disappointment," I say, taunting him. I see the anger rise in him and, I swear I see flames flicker behind his eyes.

"Do not push me, Adelaide. You will not like what you find if you do."

"As if there's anything worse you could do to me," I say with defiance.

His eyes narrow and he leans closer to the bars. I can see the darkness inside him. It's thinly veiled as he tries to mask his true self from me, but it's slipping, and I can see right in. If it were anyone else, I'd think there was beauty in the darkness, but not here. Here there is just shadows.

"I have done things you cannot even comprehend, you stupid child. I haven't even broken the surface of what I'm willing to do to get what I want," he threatens in a chilling voice.

"Threats are nothing. Actions speak louder than words, and you've got nothing. Try and intimidate one of your weaklings' old man. You obviously need me for something, so your words are empty."

He roars. The walls shake and pieces of the ceiling shower down around me. His wings break free, so black they almost look like shadows, and smoke starts to rise from his skin. He's more wild than when Kaden showed me his true self. Cole's wings are bigger than any I've seen. Michael & Kaden's wings were beautiful, but Cole's, somehow they have the opposite effect. They just add to his darkness.

"Do not push me, little girl," he growls. Livvy and Logan rush towards us down the hall led by Suki.

"Syre, you must calm down," Suki says quietly, keeping her distance. He spins to face them, and they each look to the ground. Pathetic. I look at Cole, his chest rising and falling with each ragged breath he takes. He slowly composes himself and returns to his previous form.

"What's up, Pops? Can't keep your cool? Tut tut! Say, do I get a pair of those fine and dandy wings or did I draw the short straw in the genetic lottery?"

He says nothing but he scowls at me before storming away with Suki in tow.

"Way to go, Addie. Nothing like pissing off the boss on his first day back, and I thought you were smarter than that," Livvy says to me. I can't tell if she's pissed off at me, or terrified of having to deal with Cole.

"Livvy, shut it. If you expect me to be all freaking peachy keen after everything, you can do one. The least he deserves is to feel some of the anger I feel," I snarl at her.

"Guys, please don't fight," Logan pleads. I roll my eyes at him and lay back down on this poor excuse of a bed. He says something to Livvy, which I don't quite catch before he leaves us alone.

"Get your ass up, you stupid bitch," Livvy says angrily. "Before you made such good friends with the boss, he asked me to get you cleaned up," she says to me with a bitchy smirk painted across her face. For the first time in my life, I want to beat it off of her. It looks so wrong. I give her the finger and stand up as she unlocks the door. She might look like Liv, but the bitch who is standing by the door is not my Livvy. My Livvy died that night at the Academy.

Whoever this is… well, she's a tool.

I walk past her and out of the door. The thought of running crosses my mind until I see the ridiculous amount of muscle waiting down the hall. There's two of them, and they look like total meat heads.

"What's up, Liv? Didn't think you could handle me on your own? You need Thing One and Thing Two to back you up?" I laugh, and her face twists with anger. She grabs my arm hard, making me stumble a little before I catch myself.

"I'd have no problem ripping out your throat! They're here for you; to make sure you don't hurt yourself. There's a lot more here for you to worry about than me," she snarls.

She drags me through corridors and up staircases before opening a door leading to a bedroom. It looks untouched and unused – almost clinically clean. Weird.

She pulls me straight through to the bathroom and points at the shower.

"Sort out your shit! I'll be waiting outside, and don't take forever," she says before leaving the room and closing the door. I let out a sigh of relief. Just the sight of a shower makes me far happier than it should. I turn the tap and peel off my clothes, which are crusty with dirt, and leave them in the corner. Steam fills the room, and I feel my entire body start to sag. Climbing under the hot water feels like heaven, even if the uncountable cuts I have received at the hand of Micah and his favourite knife sting like hell under the heat of the water. I lean forward against the wall, watching the blood and dirt run from my body and down the drain. Tears run down my face, disguised by the water running down my body. I don't know why I'm crying; I just know that I need to. I've resisted thinking too much about everything. Xander. Home. Everything I could potentially lose. In this one moment of solitude, I let it all out. The frustration, the anger. I cry for my lost friends, and all of the things I wish could be. I need to clear my mind before I face whatever my next fuck-tastic torture is. I need to be strong and these feelings, these regrets are a weakness.

A loud bang on the door startles me, and I slip, grabbing onto the shower rail to stay on my feet.

"Come on, Addie, don't make me come in there. We both know you won't enjoy it. Hurry the hell up," she shouts.

"Get a grip, Liv. I'm showering off a shitload of grime here. You can give me at least another ten minutes," I shout back. I grab a bottle of shampoo from the shelf and run it through my hair. It's grown so long. I need to get it cut; it's becoming almost unmanageable. *Not really high on the priority list right now, Ads*, I think to myself before laughing out loud. Maybe I'm losing my mind? I stand under the hot water for another five minutes just to piss Liv of. Screw it, what do I care. I'm going to be kept here either way. The door flies open and Liv stomps in; her arms crossed over her chest.

"Seriously, Addie? Get out of the god damn shower before I pull you out," she says, throwing towels at the door. "I've got you some clothes, but if you don't hurry up, I'll throw them out and you can go naked."

I roll my eyes at her and turn off the shower. I make no attempt to cover myself up. It's not the first time she's seen me this way, but it *is* the first time I've looked so emaciated; the ribs showing under my skin, and my muscle tone has faded. Not surprising considering everything I've been through. Despite her hard act, her eyes flit away guiltily and she leaves muttering something under her breath that I don't quite catch. I dress quickly before following her out of the door. Thing One and Thing

Two are standing outside the door, and Liv is nowhere in sight. *Maybe I could make it out of here? There's no way these guys have any sort of speed with all that bulk... right?*

Who am I kidding?

I retreat back inside the room. I barely have the strength to stay upright let alone run. The despair grips me again and it takes all I have to push it back down. I will not break now. I have too much to lose outside of here.

Sliding down the wall, my knees meeting my chest, I wrap my arms around myself, desperate for human warmth. With my head on my knees, I think on all the reasons to survive this. Xander. Rose. Dimitri. Hell, even Kaden, Michael, and Celeste. Each cut and sore on my body pinches, giving me a reason to survive and destroy all those who thought they could do this to me, to those I love, to the whole goddamn world. I don't know exactly what Coles plan is, but if what I've learnt in the past is true, whatever it is won't be good for anyone but him. His side cannot be allowed to succeed, and if they have to die, then so be it. Even Livvy if it comes to it. She's the whole reason I'm here.

Resolve builds inside me. There is no way I'm not getting out of here.

"Stay strong Addie. We can survive this." I hear a voice in my head that sounds like mine but doesn't belong to me. *Just what I need. Voices in my head. Awesome!*

"We've got this Addie. You just need to be strong for a little while longer. I'm here. You're not alone anymore. I'll keep you safe."

When I lift my head Logan is crouched in front of me. I must have fallen asleep.

"How are you holding up, Addie?" he asks.

"About as well as can be expected."

He sits beside me and wraps an arm around me. "I'm sorry that it's all come to this," he says.

"What happened to her?" I ask quietly.

"You mean Liv?"

I nod, not wanting to stop the flow of him speaking. I need answers.

He chewed at his thumb thinking for a moment. Silently, I urged him to carry on. He glanced around and took a deep breath before saying, "When we got here, she was exactly how you'd remember her. I don't know everything that happened exactly, but there are monsters that live here Addie. Some of them are dead now, but I couldn't save her from them all. They did things to her - things I will never say out loud - because she was weak.

"When she arrived she was sweet and pure and innocent, and they wanted all of it. They wanted to be the ones to claim it; be the one responsible for breaking her. Cole saved her, but not after something had changed in her. He found her after they'd finished playing with her – they just tossed her away. Cole's wrath extended across

33

the house, making each of those who made her suffer, suffer in a worse kind. None of them are here anymore. And Liv, well she's not who she used to be, and I don't think she could be even if she tried. I'm not making excuses for her, but I can't even imagine... I'm not excusing her behaviour, Ads. She's being a bitch, but maybe now you'll understand her a little better."

I'm in shock. I never would have imagined. I couldn't have. And the fact Cole stopped it all, that he saved her – I'm not sure what to make of that either. I sit and ponder the possibilities, daydream about what could have been. Logan sits beside me in silence, letting it all sink in.

After a while, I feel him get up and walk away from me, followed by the sound of the door closing.

I'm alone again.

Chapter Three

XANDER

It's been three months since I left. A month and a half since I got back, and no-one seems to have any hint of an idea where Addie's gone or when she left. Bloody hell! I don't have a clue where else to look. She has no-one else here anymore and after the way we left things, it wouldn't surprise me if she's just taken off, just to piss me off.

I run my hands through my hair for the hundredth time, trying not to pull it out. I'm sat in our kitchen with no clue of what to do next. Dimitri doesn't think she's left, and if anyone knows her better than I do, it's him.

Luckily I love him like a brother so I know I have nothing to worry about. The whole team has been out searching for her. Christ, I even sent my best trackers, Zero and Gunner, with Salene out to other territories looking for her. No-one has seen her. There are whispers, but nothing concrete. I slam my hands down on the oak table I bought for her, regretting it as soon as I hear the wood splinter. Christ. I can't handle this. I need her back. I need to know she's okay. And if the rumours are true, if Cole has her, then I'm not sure she's okay at all.

It kills me to think on how long he could have had her while I was away on that stupid recon mission, which ended up being a total waste of time! History feels like it is repeating itself again – and again, I have no control over it. If I was a better man, I'd hide it better, but I keep lashing out at those around me even though it's not their fault. The frustration and desperation inside of me is building and I can't seem to stop it. For centuries, I've had a handle on myself. I was the definition of calm and collected, but then she came into my life. Ever since I fell hard in love with her, something inside me unlocked; unleashing emotions I never thought I'd feel. And it's too late now to put the cork back in the bottle. I've never known happiness like I feel when I'm with her. If I had to trade an eternity of suffering to have her in my arms again, it would be worth it.

I know what I have to do, but doing it means unlocking the secret I swore to keep all those years ago. It means putting so many people in danger to save her, but I'd walk through the fires of Hell if it meant saving her. *I will get her back if it's the last thing I do.*

I'm pacing the room, waiting for everyone to arrive. They're all due here any minute with news of their latest search, and for the first time, I can remember, my patience is wearing thin. Finally, the door opens, and they walk in with a solemn look on each of their faces.

"I'm assuming this means no-one has good news?" I say, terser than I mean to, but I don't seem to have much control over my anger right now.

"The only thing we're hearing is what we've already heard. She's with Cole. No-one seems to know how long she's been with him, or if she went willingly. We have no solid information and no-one from his side is talking. Whatever's going on, it's being kept quiet, and that worries me," Dimitri says.

He rarely worries; he's as level-headed as I am, which sets my protective instincts into overdrive. *What does he want with her?*

"If this is all we have, then I have no choice but to take action. I need to visit someone, in the meantime, go back to The Academy and make sure the guard is on alert. I'll come and find you all later." The edge in my voice obvious. I see that they are unsettled by my high emotion but they are loyal. They nod at me, accepting their orders before leaving the house – all but Dimitri; the most loyal of them all.

"You know I'm going with you, right? Addie is like a sister to me, Xander.

I go to protest, my heart raging that he has no right to claim he feels even a drop of the love I feel for her, but it isn't true. He does love her as a brother – and that love is

37

powerful. He's right: she needs us both, and he's going to find out the truth sooner or later.

"Fine, you can come, but whatever you hear, you need to keep to yourself," I say. I see a flash of question across his brow. "I mean it, Dimitri; it's that, or you don't come with me."

He nods. 'Unless it's something that can help her."

"If it can help her, I'll use it myself," I snap.

At the splendorous gates of The Valoire Palace, the guards see me and open up; I can see the questions in their eyes. I only come here if something is wrong, unless there is a State celebration. If only they knew.

Pulling on this particular string is going to unravel a lot of truths for a lot of people. Lives are going to change, and I can't say it will all be for the better, but I have no other options. I need the Queen's help if I'm going to save her daughter.

A wave of guilt suddenly slams through me. Guilt for not protecting her, for blurring the lines – for falling in love with Addie. I'd never change it, not for a minute, but the loyal streak in me, the one I've battled with this last year, the one that told me everything I've done is wrong, that's the one that's front and centre.

We pull the car up in front of the imposing palace doors and get out. Dimitri follows swiftly behind me. I hand the keys to the new kid working the valet service. The wonder on his face is not something I'm fazed by. The palace looks like something from the imagination of a child; light coloured stone glimmers in the sunlight, as if covered in glitter. With rounded turrets at each end of the front wall, the palace stretches out on either side of us, almost as far as the eye can see before being taken over by the wilderness of the forest that surrounds it. Being the head of my House means I come across the palace reasonably often be it because all hell has broken loose or when certain Fae come to visit, especially when they're from other territories.

I walk with purpose towards the throne room, no-one stops me. Being known has its advantages. The guards at the doors of the throne room open them without any kind of exchange of pleasantries. It is clear I mean business. My arrival is announced before I even get to the door. King Kellan and Queen Eolande are sat on their respective thrones, the room buzzes with activity still recovering from the Frosthearts being here when they came to collect Rose after Addie saved her, I'm sure.

"Xander Bane," King Kellan bellows, "and what did we do to merit sure a rare visit?"

39

"Your Highness, I request a private meeting with Queen Eolande," I say bowing down on one knee.

"Xander, get up. You know you don't need to do that," Eolande says, her voice so raspy it almost sounds like a whisper. She stands and joins me, linking her arm with mine. "You can always come and see me, my dearest one. Let's go to my garden room."

She leads me out of the hall, Dimitri on our heels, leaving a suspicious looking Kellan sat on his throne. Appearances mean a lot to the Fae, he would never let his distaste for me, and my kind be known. He's an old purist. As far as he's concerned, unless you're a Fae of noble blood, you are not worthy of his time.

The garden room is room made from glass, and it takes up one entire end of the palace. It's so big you could easily get lost in it, especially as the greenery is almost more wild and luscious than what's to be found out there in the actual forest. Small humming birds flit around, hovering orchid to orchid, and causing a momentary distraction. It's a magical space, and reflects everything Eolande is.

Eolande walks us to a table and chairs set out for tea. She pours us each a cup of the rich Chinese tea before sitting down herself.

"Now then, Xander, what brings you all the way here?" she asks nervously.

"Your daughter," I say, blunt and to the point. Her face pales and she places her cup down on its saucer shakily.

The shock on Dimitri's face is not hidden either, but he says nothing.

"My… my daughter? You watched over her? Where is she? Is she okay?" she asks, looking hesitantly at Dimitri, I smile at her to reassure her that she can trust him.

"I do. You've met her, and she has grown into an extraordinary young woman."

Wonder and happiness drift across her face until she looks in my eyes and realizes something is wrong.

"What is it Xander?" she asks.

"She's been taken. Again. Except this time, all we have are whispers. I need your help to find her, Eolande."

"Taken! Who would do such a thing?" she gasps.

"From everything we're hearing, it's Cole. Do you have any idea why he would be interested in her?" I ask.

Her face falls and she gathers it in her hands, crying, "I knew this would come back to haunt me." She raises her head, meets my eye and I see that a fire has burned out her tears. The shock and fear have transformed into something fierce. "That stupid son of a bitch never could learn to let things go!"

My shock at her language is evident, and she laughs bitterly, "Xander don't look at me like that; I'm a queen, not a saint."

"Sorry, Ma'am."

She looks out of the window and towards the forest – thinking deeply, and I can see she's drilling a dark well.

41

After several moments of internal battle, her eyes return to mine, and despite the recent angry outburst, I see a film of tears has returned across her eyes.

"I suppose I need to tell you the whole story." She sighs. "You'd both better get comfortable – it's a complicated one.

"The secret I told you all those years ago wasn't the complete truth, Xander. I'm sorry for that, but I wanted to protect my daughter as much as I could. Aeveen isn't half Fae, half human; it wasn't a human male I had an affair with, it was Cole."

My eyes widen so much that the bright sunlight feels like a stab from a knife. "Cole?" The name shoots from my mouth before I can stop it."

Queen Eolande is not impressed by my judgement, but to be fair, I'm not sure she's standing on solid ground. She's humiliated and her cheeks are flushed with shame. She hurries to explain, "I was caught up in an unhappy marriage, and his charm was like a breath of fresh air. I knew it was wrong. I knew I couldn't trust him, but I couldn't help myself – it's hard to explain; it was an almost elemental draw. We snuck around for a little over two years, but I ended the affair once I realized what he was really after."

The shadow that flits across her eye tells me she loved him. She actually loved him! And he hurt her.

"He wanted a child," she continues, "but not just any child, he wanted the child from the prophecies: half Fae, half Fallen. Twice as strong as both, and twice as powerful. It wasn't me he loved; he was just power hungry. It was weeks later, after I'd ended everything, that I discovered I was pregnant. You can imagine my surprise, what with the difficulty my kind have with conception, and with my own marriage being barren. The idea hadn't even cross my mind. Other than the prophecies of old, it is not even thought possible, but it was, and I was pregnant. I hid my pregnancy from everyone but you, Xander. But I couldn't tell you the whole truth. What she was, what she could be…

"If the truth gets out, the other Fae families won't accept her. They'll want her put to death, and they won't be shy about it, Xander. That's why I asked you to hide her among the humans, why I didn't tell you the truth. I hoped she wouldn't manifest any power and I bound her just in case. I hoped and prayed each day that she wouldn't be the child from the prophecy. She was never meant to find out who she was. This world, the world of the Royal Fae, isn't one I'd wish on my daughter. Especially not when she is a hybrid."

I sit back, trying to take in everything Queen Eolande just revealed. I've heard of the prophecy, we all have, of the hybrid child. The Reborn. A Fae warrior with the power to bring us to our knees. The warrior who would have the power to turn the world we know into nothing more than ash and to devastate the Earth.

"Are you truly telling me Addie is the one the prophecy speaks of?" I ask.

"Addie? I like that name. It's fitting for Aeveen. And I don't know, but Cole clearly thinks she is."

"It would explain the great lengths he's gone through to capture her," Dimitri says. I can already see him plotting and strategizing. He's been quiet, but that's what he does best.

"It would," Queen Eolande says. "As you know, Xander, this is not the first time she has been taken. It's easy enough to assume Kaden captured her on behalf of Cole, even if just to open her eyes to the reality of her world, so accepting the rest of whatever lies he's spun her are more believable. We need to find her, and quickly. If everything that's been said here is the truth, and she is the one from the prophecy, we need to get her back before he taints her mind with his twisted truths."

"And what if she believes any lies he spins her? What if she sides with him?" Dimitri asks. "Cole hasn't lied to her like we have, he hasn't kept things from her – even if it was for her own good. If what you think is right, then Kaden has already proved to her that we've been dishonest with her, she could trust Cole easily. We both know how persuasive he can be."

"Xander, Dimitri, you need to save my daughter – not just because she is my daughter, but because she has the potential to destroy everything we know if played wrongly. I will deal with the consequences of accepting her as my daughter, and I will work on the other Fae families. I will do whatever I can to help and give you whatever resources you need."

"Xander, we're going to need help to find her," Dimitri says after exhaling a long breath of disbelief. Perhaps I should have given him some forewarning; the poor guy's head must be spinning – but ever the professional strategic brains, he turns to things he can understand – military tactics. "The Valoire tracers can't find her – they're some of the best in the land. It's clear we need more help – help from a different source."

"I know, Dimitri, but we have to be careful who we ask, who we trust. It could be dangerous for Addie," I say gritting my teeth with frustration. I'm still trying to get my own head around Queen Eolande's lies. Things would have been so much easier to manage if she had just been honest with me from the start.

"I know. I'm not saying we ask just anyone," he replies, putting his hand on my shoulder.

His unswerving support softens me. "Did you have anyone in mind?" I ask.

"Actually, yes. While the Valoire tracers are busy, they're not the only Fae we know. Rose is a Dream Walker. She could reach out to Addie. They've done it before so the connection is already there. We both know if Rose knew what had happened, she'd demand to help anyway. She loves Addie, and you know how she longs for a cause to channel that fierce fighting skill into. Personally, I wouldn't want to risk pissing her off by not getting her on board."

Dimitri chuckles and relief runs through me. He's right. I hadn't even thought of Rose. She thinks of Addie like a sister if anyone would be willing to sacrifice, to help us save Addie it would be her.

"You're a genius, Dimitri!"

"Oh, I know," Dimitri says laughing. "No-one is ever going to believe you admitted it, though!"

I laugh at him because we both know he's right. I'm not sure how I'd get through this without him. If I lose her... It's not worth thinking about.

"Guess we better get things planned, brother. It seems I'm going home, and England is a long way from here."

"Too right, thank god for transporters. Queen Valoire said one was available, right?" Dimitri asks. Transporter Fae are Fae who can travel anywhere in the world and take up to five additional people with them. Since we no longer run planes, transporters make life much easier especially in instances like this.

"Yes, she has two for us, should we need them later. For now, we just need to let the rest of them know what we have planned. Can I leave that to you while I liaise with the Fae?"

"Sure thing. What time do we leave?"

"In about four hours, so we don't have long. It might be worth grabbing a few minutes' sleep, too; I have a feeling it's going to be a long and exhausting few days."

Dimitri mumbles something as he climbs in the car but the rest of the journey back to The Academy is quiet. I think of little else but getting her back. I only hope Rose can help us. My mind reels with the possibility of the things Addie's going through – Cole's not known for his soft and fuzzy side. My knuckles turn white with my grip on the steering wheel and I try to restrain myself before I snap the damn thing. I hate feeling this bloody useless. *I am never letting her out of my god damn sight again!* I try to calm the fire rising inside of me; I picture her face, recall her kicking my arse in her lessons, her feisty nature challenging me at every turn. I hope she's giving whoever has her a headache. She can be a wildcat. The thought makes me laugh causing some of the tension to leave me. Dimitri is wise enough not to enquire.

The Academy appears on the horizon. I tell myself that it won't be long until she's be back in my arms where she belongs. I pull into the underground parking garage and put the car back in its spot. Dimitri heads off immediately to get things sorted, and I head to the Head Keeper's office. I try not to deal with her too often, the woman gives me the heebie jeebies. I knock on her door and no-one answers so I leave a note with her secretary and head back to my room to get my gear together before taking my own advice and grabbing some sleep.

Just as I drop my packed bag on the desk of my office Dimitri walks in followed by two Fae women.

"Ladies, please meet Xander Bane," Dimitri says gesturing towards me.

I walk over and shake their hands. They're very young. "It's lovely to meet you both," I say, trying to smile, despite my misgivings.

"The pleasure is ours," the smaller of the two says giggling. Both have fiery red hair and ivory pale skin and I wonder if they are sisters. They look almost ethereal. "My name is Liana," she says, "and this is my sister, Eevara. Queen Eolande asked us to assist you in your travels."

"Yes, you know where we are going?" I ask.

"To the old monarch, the home of the Frosthearts," Eevara, the taller of the two says. Her voice is so soft that it's more like a whisper. She looks up at me with her wide green eyes, wonder on her face. I am used to this kind of reaction from the Fae youth. They know my name, and I've heard some of the stories they tell about the great warrior I'm rumoured to be. Hearing about my fictional jaunts makes me laugh frequently. My favourite has to be the one where I fought the last dragon and won, making them extinct.

"Exactly. Hopefully, from there on we will be fine, and you will be able to return home," I say, unable to hide the frustration I feel at Eolande having sent two such delicate creatures to assist us. I don't know what she thinks we're about to do exactly, but taking on Cole isn't exactly a day out at the park. They seem innocent enough, but I suppose Queen Eolande wouldn't have sent them to me if she didn't trust them.

They giggle again and Dimitri rolls his eyes behind them. Just what we need, more children to look after.

"Are you ladies ready to go?" I ask. The sooner I can send them back home, the better. They nod before linking hands and grabbing onto Dimitri and I grab my bag and close my eyes ready for the gut churn I know is coming.

I hate transporting.

We arrived roughly ten minutes ago and Dimitri has been throwing up since. I've only just managed to keep it together. I sent the Fae back home. I know for a fact the Frosthearts have more experienced transporters; the more experienced, the smoother the ride, and I sure as shit am not going through that again. Dimitri makes his way back towards me, paler than normal, which I didn't think was actually possible.

"Never again!" he says, his gag reflex still not fully calmed as he heaves. I slap him on the back.

"Man up. We've got shit to do!"

He grumbles as I stride ahead towards the entrance of Frostheart Palace. The guards scramble as they see us coming. Queen Eolande has sent word to Nico Baldisseri, the Head of the Baldisseri House, and the Royal Fae guard here. The doors open and I see Nico stood there, the strain obvious in his posture. He stands at nearly seven-foot-tall, a giant of a man, with a bald head that shines in the dim light. He's a powerhouse, and built like one, too. He wears his trademark full length cloak, with wolf fur along the neckline. The rest of him is clad in black – a series of shadows.

"Xander, it is nice to see you again, old friend," he says with a tight smile as he grabs my arm and we shake.

"Indeed it is, I just wish it were better circumstances."

Nico and Dimitri catch up as he leads us to a drawing room where Rose and Benny are waiting for us. They haven't been briefed as yet, that's been left for me. We walk down the silent hall. The tension is thick in the air and it's almost suffocating. I don't want to tell Rose that Addie is missing, not after everything they went through together already. I don't want her to blame me, even though she should. Just knowing I failed Addie again kills me. Nico opens the door to the drawing room and I can hear Benny and Rose's laughter, I feel bad that I'm about to extinguish it. I walk into the room and see them both sat down with a third person I didn't expect – Kristian Frostheart.

"Xander! Dimitri!" Rose squeals, jumping up and hugging us both in turn. "What are you guys doing here? Is Addie here, too? I've missed her! Please say she's coming, too!" she says excitedly, her innocent eyes searching behind us. I give her a small smile and Benny stands and touches her waist, knowing by instinct that something is wrong.

"Xander. Dimitri," Benny says nodding to us both. "Rose, honey, I think you better sit down."

51

"Xander Bane, you old dog! What brings you across the pond? Missing home?" Kristian asks, wrapping me in a hug and slapping my back. "Dimitri! It has been a long time!"

"I think you guys should all sit down," I say in a solemn voice. I watch as each of them sit on the sofas in front of me, Dimitri and Nico each standing on either side of the door behind me.

"There's no easy way to tell you this, but Addie is missing."

"Missing?! What do you mean she's missing?" Rose asks.

"Calm down Rose, getting upset isn't going to help Addie." Benny reaches out to soothe her and she leans back into him.

"I mean she is *missing*. Shortly after you both returned home, I was sent on a mission with my Elite team. We were gone for a month and a half. When I returned home there was no sign of Addie. We have searched since then with no luck. We have no solid leads on where she is, and no Fae tracers can get a lock on her. We have no idea when she was taken, or by whom. We've heard whispers, but that's all we have."

"Holy crap!" Rose says, brushing away Benny's arms and jumping up from the sofa. Rose has a fierce spirit and she's wired. I brace myself. "You've been home for what two months? And it took you this long to come and tell me!

52

Are you freaking kidding me? I can help you, bloody men!" she rants, pacing in front of the sofa.

"Rose," I say, my hands extended in submission. "Please, that's why we're here now. We want you to speak to her, to find out where she is – to find out what's going on," I say softly, feeling foolish for not having done this sooner. She's right to call me out on it.

"Could this be dangerous for Rose?" Benny asks, the concern obvious.

"Shut up, Benny. If it wasn't for Addie, I wouldn't be here. Of course I'm doing it. I'll be fine." She shoots back.

Damn, you can tell she spent a lot of time around my girl. I smile at her and she hugs me again.

"Sorry Xander," she says, "I didn't mean to yell at you, but she's Addie... you know. I need her to be okay. It's not your fault." She says to me, before looking over my shoulder. She walks over to D and hugs him too.

"It's not your fault either." She says. "And I know that she wouldn't blame either of you. So suck it up, and let's find our girl."

CRASH

Chapter Four

ADDIE

I'm running through a forest. I have no idea where the hell I am, but I know I'm being chased, and I'm terrified. My pulse is racing as I run through the trees. I try to push the branches out of the way, but I'm only in shorts and a vest and I'm getting cuts all over my body. I keep running and I can hear it, whatever it is, getting closer. Some dark force. Something terrible, catching up to me and I push myself to go even faster. The adrenaline spikes, the cold, which was seeping into my bones withdraws and is replaced with nothing but the fight to keep going. There's a clearing ahead and I push harder. I don't know why, but I just know I'll be safe there.

Coming to the edge of the clearing, I slow down. A shimmering of sorts has caught my attention. I put my hand out in front of me and I can feel the energy on my fingertips, I push my hand through it. Before I know what is happening, I've been pulled through it fully and I can hear my own scream of surprise.

It takes me a minute to clear my head and orientate myself. I'm back at the mansion, in the room Kaden kept me in.

"Addie?"

"Rose?" I spin around and see her stood there. This can't be real

"Thank goodness I found you, Addie, I've been trying for hours. They wanted me to stop for the night, but I knew I had to find you!"

"Is this real?" I ask, still doubting my frame of mind. She rushes towards me and wraps me up in a hug. The relief is real as I slump into her and my knees give way.

"I'm really here, Addie," she says hugging me. Tears run down her face, too. "I'm so glad you're okay. Everyone is worried sick! Are you really okay? Where are you?"

"I don't know. Livvy turned up the night Xander left, the night you left. I really thought she was back. That she was okay. I was so relieved she was alive. It never occurred to me not to trust her. It's Liv…."

"What do you mean? I thought you said Liv was dead?"

"I thought she was, too, but she's alive, Rose – Logan, too. They're both here. I have no idea how long I've been here. There's no light where they keep me, no windows. I don't even know if it's night or day," I say to her.

The stunned look on her face doesn't surprise me. Shock is better than pity.

"I can't believe they're alive, Addie. What you must be feeling and going through. I'm so sorry I left you!"

"It's not your fault, Rose." I say, tugging down on the long sleeves on my top. She sees me and raises her eyebrows, questioning me.

"It's nothing. I just… I don't know how much longer I'm going to last here. I think I'm losing my mind. I'm not even sure this is real," I admit. My grasp on reality is slipping, and I'm pretty sure that hearing someone else inside my head is not a good sign.

"Talk to me, Addie. I'm here now," she says. I can see the pity creeping into her eyes and I hate it.

"You really want to know? You want to know that they hurt me, torture me every single day and I have no idea why? That their butcher, Micah, the sadistic fuck, seems to get off every time I scream," I say. "I tried so hard not to scream at the beginning, but there comes a point where it's impossible not to. You want to know that I'm weak? That it hurts so much that sometimes I pass out? That I'm surrounded by Vampyrs and Demons, and I can't trust a single person around me. Not even Liv or Logan. I never thought I'd say that." It all rushes out of me in one long stream and I can't stop it.

"They tortured me so badly that I left my own body. I was watching myself from a distance, and someone else

was there inside me. Whilst she was there, I felt nothing. The relief was so strong that death was appealing. Of course, you don't want to know any of that, but this probably isn't real so it doesn't matter anyway."

Tears run down Rose's and she flies towards me, wrapping her arms around me. She pulls back from me but keeps my hand tightly clasped in hers.

"This is real, Addie; you feel this?" she asks squeezing my hand. "I'm real and I swear we are coming for you. Xander and Dimitri are both here with me, Benny too. You just need to hold on a little longer until we get to you. I need you to hold on. I need you to promise you'll wait for us."

I nod, keeping my head lowered. Hope isn't something I can hold onto right now.

"I've got to go right now, Addie, but I'll be back, I promise. I love you," she says before she flickers away from my sight.

I look up at the sky confused as my surroundings change, I'm still here in the ball of energy, but everything outside has changed. It's dark now, stars scattered across the night sky, the moon shines down so bright it illuminates my little patch of forest. I hear a wolf howl in the distance, the sound of night birds rustling around in the leaves. I lay back and close my eyes, enjoying this small bit of peace. If this is the last peace I ever feel, it's kind of perfect. Something is near me, and I open my eyes, looking around the edges of the meadow. The bushes move and I stand quickly. I thought I was safe here. So much for peace, I should've known I don't get peace, not even in my sleep. The noise of snapping twigs makes me zone in on the bushes directly to my left, and that's when I see a wolf – and he's huge.

He dips his head submissively to me as if asking permission. This is beyond crazy. I nod my head because it feels as if he's waiting for me to respond. He pads towards me slowly, stopping just in front of me before laying down and watching me. He's waiting for me to close the distance. As I step closer to him, I hear him whine, quietly hurrying me. His mane looks so soft, so fluffy and shiny. The black of his fur reflects the silver of the moon, making him look almost ghostlike. I can't resist reaching out and touching him. I run my hand through his fur, and I was right. It's so soft.

"Do not be afraid of me child," he says inside my head. I gasp and step back. What the hell! He whines at me again, encouraging me to come back to him. Hesitantly, I reach out to him.

"I will not hurt you. I am here to help you."

"Who are you?" I ask. This has to be real right? Surely I'm not this crazy. Right?

"My name is Kasabian Narayama, but you can call me Kas. I am the Alpha of the Hunter pack. I heard your plea for help and so I am here."

59

I'm stiff all over. I open my eyes slowly and take in my surroundings. I'm still in the room Liv left me in, tucked into myself against the wall. What a way to fall asleep. I stretch out before my dream comes back to me and I'm filled with sadness. I don't dare hope it was real. Hope is dangerous, but seeing Rose helped me remember myself a little. I'm not some helpless little girl; I got us out of a situation just like this once before already. There's no reason I can't save myself. I stand up and look around the room, spotting a tray of food on the dresser across the room. I look around but there's definitely no-one else in here with me. *"You should eat. We need the strength."* I look around searching for the source of the voice, before I realize it's the same voice I heard before – the one inside my own head.

"Who are you?" I ask.

"I am you – kind of. My name is Aeveen, and we are one. Or at least, we were meant to be. I've been here forever, watching you, learning, listening.*"*

"Okay… so that's more than a little creepy – and it makes no sense."

"I'm the other part of you, Addie. Now eat. Please"

I've officially lost my mind, but whoever she is, she's right, I do need to eat. My stomach rumbles and it hurts. I can't remember the last time I ate. I move slowly towards the dresser so as not to alert anyone who might be outside that I'm awake. My mouth waters when I see the cheeseburger along with some fries. Popping one into my mouth, I relish the sensations – so salty and still warm! I groan with satisfaction before picking up the burger and taking a bite. I scoff it down, feeling sick afterwards, but it was so worth it!

"That was probably a bad idea. You know that, right?" the voice says.

Now even the voice in my head judges me. Screw it, I love cheese burgers. I pace back and forth in the room, trying to burn off the nervous energy I feel coursing through me. This might be a nicer cage, but it's still a cage.

I spin as the door opens and Liv walks in, staring at me as if I were some kind of wild animal.

"Get your shit together, Addie. I've got to take you back."

"Back? Home?" I ask, the hope so heavy it crushes me. Her harsh laugh brings me hurtling back down to reality.

"Oh please, this isn't like when you were with Kaden, Addie. Cole is the real deal. He wants you, I have no idea why, but he's fixated on you."

61

"That's probably because I'm his daughter," I say, trying to throw her. The shock on her face informs me I have succeeded. She attempts to hides it, her mask flicks back quickly.

"Yes, I suppose that could be why. Anyway, you're going back downstairs as per Daddy Dearest's orders."

I step back from her, shaking my head. "I'm not going back down to that hell hole, Liv."

"You don't have a choice, Addie; I don't want to hurt you. I'm just following orders."

I laugh at her. "As if I'm going to believe that. Like I'd ever believe a word you say again. Fool me once, shame on you. Fool me twice… yeah not going to happen."

"Don't make me force you, Addie. I'd really rather not hurt you. Pick your battles. You're going to need your strength."

Chapter Five

XANDER

The waiting is torture. I can do nothing but sit here and wait for Rose to wake up. When she came back last time, she pleaded with me to do something more to find Addie. She told me everything Addie had said to her, and every word was like a knife, cutting me deep. I can't even imagine what she's going through. Having Livvy betray her like that after just discovering she was alive again, finding out Logan is alive, that Cole is her father. The fallout from that little tid bit was just another small echo of the chaos we're all dealing with, I think with everything else going on, it almost seemed insignificant at this point. All of this alone would be enough to handle, but knowing what she's endured since they took her. That was two days ago, and now I'm waiting again, for even the smallest sign that she's still alive, that she's okay.

What makes it all worse is they took her on the day I left. They were waiting for me to leave. They didn't even give me a chance to protect her. I need to make it up to her. I need HER. I punch the stone wall and pieces shower around me, the edge to my frustration has barely gone. Dimitri watches me from the other side of the room with no judgement. I know he feels the same way I do in this moment. I'm walking a dangerous line right now. I need to feed, but I can't, not until I know she's okay.

Benny is stood like a sentry at the end of Rose's bed, the tension in the room is palpable. Rose wanted to try to reach Addie again tonight in hopes of reasoning with her, trying to persuade her that Cole is messing with her mind. I hear a gasp and turn to see Rose awake and in Benny's arms, sobbing.

"Oh, Benny, it's so horrible. What they're doing to her. I can't even…." She pauses, trying to catch her breath. "I could feel it. Every single bit of her pain, her subconscious was so riddled with it. She's so broken, I could barely break free," she cries.

"What do you mean? What changed?" I shout, startling her, the anger and bloodlust starting to loosen my control.

"They're torturing her, Xander," she cries. "I only managed to get through because she passed out from the pain. I didn't get to speak to her, I could only sift through bits of her memories, and feel her emotions. The despair took my breath away, but the pain, it was soul shattering. They're breaking her, and I have no idea why. All I got from her memory was that she had disappointed Cole, and this was her punishment. We have to find her, Xander and quickly, otherwise we're going to lose her."

Her warning takes my breath away and for a minute, I think I'm going to crumble. Then my anger takes control of my body. I clench my fists so hard that I feel my bones creak under the pressure. I need to get out of here and hit something. Hit someone. I rip open the door and head towards the gym. It's been years since I've been here but I trained here, and nothing much has changed.

There are a few people in the gym already. Guards doing their daily training, some Fae just working out because they want to. I head straight for the empty punch bag. I don't bother to wrap my hands; I need to feel this. I hit the bag again and again, feeling the leather crack under my fists, feeling the skin on my knuckles break and split before it heals almost instantly. The rhythm becomes hypnotic and soothing as I beat out my frustration, the feeling of helplessness subsiding slightly as the numbness takes over for a while.

I have no idea how long it has taken before the bag finally gives way and splits. I lift my top and wipe the sweat from my face before looking around the room and realizing I'm now alone. This helped for a while, but it all comes crashing back as soon as I stop punching. The need for her. The guilt. My failure. The surge of anger rises in me again, threatening to overwhelm me. I need to feed. I grab a quick shower before I head back upstairs to face Dimitri and Rose. I have failed them, too.

I hesitate outside of the door. I can't fail them again, and I won't. Too many people in my past have been hurt because of me – because I wasn't enough. I will save Addie, even if it means sacrificing myself.

Pushing the door open, I'm met by sullen faces. Whatever they were discussing before I entered the room ceases.

"What?" I ask.

"We need help, Xander," Dimitri says from his corner. His anger is concealed just under the surface. "You're not going to like it, but we need Kaden."

"He's right, Xander. Addie told me Kaden and Cole had a disagreement, that's why Kaden let us go. He might know where Cole is, and he genuinely seemed to like Addie. He has to help us!" she says.

Kaden is the last person in the world I want to go to for help, but their reasoning is sound. I have no reason not to do it – other than that feeling in my gut that he's going to betray us. He can't be trusted, but we've had no luck in tracing her on our own.

My brother, Kaden, is known for letting people down when it matters most. The conflict between needing to get to Addie and asking Kaden to help me, is stifling. I wrack my brain for another solution. Any other solution. God dammit, they're right. We need him.

"Bloody hell, I hate that we need to do this." I say, running my hand through my hair with exasperation. "My brother can*not* be trusted, but I don't see any other option right now." I turn to Dimitri and sigh. "It looks like we're going back home." I can see the thought of having to undergo another Fae transportation so soon has already made him queasy. I turn to Rose and Benny. "Thank you for all of your help, Rose. I can't express to you how much it means to me," I say before heading to the door, ready to pack up and get going. I don't want to waste another minute.

"Oh hell no, Xander Bane! Don't think for one minute that I'm not coming with you! Addie is my friend, and there is no way on earth you're leaving me behind!" Rose says fiercely.

It's strange seeing this side of her, but her loyalty to Addie warms me. She's going to need friends like that if she's going to survive. God I miss her.

Tracking down my brother was much easier than it should have been. Apparently, when he's not hiding the woman I love, he doesn't bother hiding his position. We sent word back to my best trackers, Gunner & Zero, before we prepared to leave the home of the Frosthearts in England with orders to find Kaden, and they found him in just a few days.

Now, I'm stood here with Dimitri trying to convince Rose that she needs to stay safe, and the best way to do that is by staying here.

She's not happy and she's full of fight. "If you think for even one second you're leaving me behind you're mistaken. There is no way I'm staying here all safe and cosy in this palace whilst my best friend is going through hell. She would risk everything for me – she's shown that. I'm coming with you and that is the end of it," she says, standing there looking every bit the royal that she is. It's that same determination I see in Addie's eyes. I sigh, knowing I'm not going to win this battle. I look over at Benny who is trying to keep from laughing.

"Fine, but Benny comes!"

That soon stops his laughter. I continue in spite of Rose's pout. "And he is fully responsible for you. He is your personal guard. We have enough to worry about without worrying about you coming along, too. I assume you have informed your parents?"

She looks at me as if I've lost my mind. "Of course I have – they're fully supportive of my decision. They know how much I love Addie and wouldn't dream of stopping me," she says defiantly.

For a rare moment, I'm speechless. Clearly having gone through what Addie and Rose did together, made both Rose stronger than I'd given her credit for – I only hoped Addie's strength was as fierce now as it was then. "Get your stuff together," I say, unwilling to openly apologise, but knowing I owed Rose one. "We leave at dawn. We've already located Kaden. We're heading straight to where he is staying. The rest of my Elite will meet us there," I say to her before turning to Benny. "If you need to bring more guards do it, but do not get in our way."

He nods before leaving the room with Rose to get ready to leave. I run my hand over my face. What I wouldn't give to just have Addie back, to have some time without all of this craziness going on around us.

And then there is the knowledge that even when I get her back, I'll have to take her to Fae court, and her mother, bringing a whole new set of problems. It hardly fills me with joy. There's little chance that when the truth comes out, our union will even be allowed let alone be blessed. That's if, after everything Addie has been through, she even wants to be with me.

Six Months ago

"Addie, are you nearly ready?" I yell from the lounge. Our new house seems to have grounded Addie, given her a place to anchor herself. She's never had somewhere to call home, and I love that I can give that to her now. I want to give her the world.

"Sheesh, man I'm coming! What's the rush? Can't wait for date night?" she says laughing as she comes halfway down the stairs in nothing but a dressing gown. Her hair and makeup are already done and I'm blown away at how lucky I am.

"You look beautiful, Addie. Maybe we should just stay in?" I say, wiggling my eyebrows at her and making her laugh again. I want to hear that sound forever. I start for her and she squeals before turning and running up the stairs. We both know her evasion is useless. I will always catch her. Always.

I reach her and pick her up, flinging her over my shoulder and she squeals, her protests at being picked up, broken by her uncontrollable giggles. I stride into the bedroom and drop her onto the bed.

"Don't you dare, Xander Bane. You promised me date night," she says putting her hands out in front of her. Her gown has opened slightly, and that's not helping change my mind.

70

"You're not really making this easy on me, babe. I mean, look at you. Why would I want to share you with the outside world?"

She blushes as she gathers up her gown. It doesn't matter how many times I see her, she always blushes, and it makes me want her even more. I stretch my arm out, grabbing onto the top of our bed frame lean over her.

"You look like a sweet little treat just waiting to be unwrapped," I tease.

"Xander, stop it!" she laughs, embarrassed. "I won't be long, then we can go out like we planned, and this little treat can be dessert," she murmurs softly, biting her lip. Dammit. Tonight is going to be one of great restraint.

"You're lucky I love you," I say kissing her. She kisses me back with so much passion, it surprises me – just as it always does. She's so innocent on the surface, but underneath, there's this rich, intoxicating hint at darkness. Her kiss deepens and I have to force myself back, leaving her breathless. Her quiet pants, mixed with her dark look of lust are close to breaking me. I roll to the side and cover my eyes with my arm.

"Get ready you minx. Later, later you're mine," I say laughing throatily.

CRASH

ADDIE

I'm back in the wretched chair, and I think I've finally lost it. Micah has stepped up his sadistic ways since he saw Aeveen. Apparently, he wants to play with her despite their last meeting. His burns have healed, but he's just crazy enough to want to endure it again.

"I keep telling you, Addie, I'm part of you. I can help you, you just need to let me in," I hear her inside my head. "It's easy, Addie, just let me take over again. You just need to let me in. I can get us out of here. I can stop all of this."

I shake my head as if that will get rid of her.

"I can't do that! I don't know how," I say out loud.

The new guards, stationed at the door, wear their faces blank, but I'm pretty sure everyone here thinks I've lost it. When Liv bought me back down here, I was weak. I begged, I cried and I pleaded for her not to put me back here – not with Micah. I was too weak to do anything else.

73

"You wouldn't be weak if you'd merge with me, Addie."

I scream and feel a rush of power. The many torture devices lined on the walls behind me, rattle, and the glass table shatters. I quiet in shock. *That wasn't me right?*

"There's so much we could do together, Addie," she says. "We will be powerful, and no-one will bend us to their will again. All of this would stop."

"SHUT UP! Shut up, shut up, shut up!" I shout, hitting my head back against the chair. I need to feel something real.

"You can't get rid of me, Addie. I am part of you. You will see soon enough, you need me. I have been kept quiet for too long. This is war. The moment to fight is coming and we will be unstoppable.

"It's a brave new world out there, Addie. We will fight to the death, but that death will not be ours."

I drop my head in defeat. She's wrong. I see no way out of here right now. I'm trying so hard to hold on, to not give up, but with every day that passes, the spark that makes me who I am dims a little more, and *she* becomes a little louder.

I worry I'm going to lose myself to her – and I know that's exactly what Cole wants. It's not me he wants, it's her. I don't know exactly why, but I can sense something in her, something dark and powerful. I'm afraid of her, and I'm even more afraid of the idea of her being connected to

Cole. It is this – and the thought of Xander – that is keeping me here rather than letting her take over. Whatever pain I have to endure, I know I must endure it. My mind recalls the time she broke through, what she did to Micah, and I know that was nothing compared to her potential. I can feel the power inside me, waiting to be unleashed – and it's demonic. I know that whoever she is, she is a demon, and I do not want to be a demon.

Micah, aside from being nifty with a torture tool, is also a master of psychological torture. He has taken great delight in telling me between the cuts and the beats that my mother was the whore of a demon, and that is why she hid me from her world. Like all Demons – rejected, until I finally embrace my demon self. They want me to give in to her. Now that I have come of age, she's ready to form, but I won't sacrifice my humanity like that. I won't toss away my capacity to ever love again – to lose the one thing in the world that makes my life worth living, Xander.

"Morning, Sunshine," Livvy says from the door. By her side is a guilty looking Logan.

"Awesome, just what I need. The welcoming committee back again."

"Well, that's just rude," Liv snarls. "And here was me thinking I'd get you out of that chair, but if you're happy with Micah…"

"Liv, don't be a bitch. Get her out of the chair," Logan says with more bite than I've heard from him yet. When she refuses, he snatches the keys from her. Kneeling down he undoes the iron locks around my ankles first, then releases the leather strips on my wrist, gently, making sure not to peel away more of my skin. I bite down on my lip to stop the screams. I am sick of screaming.

"I'm sorry, Addie," he whispers before releasing the strap across my neck. "Can you stand?" he asks. The pain I feel is reflected in his eyes. He places a hand on the back of my neck and I feel my pain start to dull. I'm amazed.

"How did you…?"

"We've all got our secrets, Ads. Just let me help when I can, okay?" he says quietly.

I nod at him before he lifts me from the chair, one arm around my back, another under my knees. Compassion isn't tolerated in this place, and Logan is pushing it.

"How touching," Liv snarks. "We've got a healing bath for you upstairs. Then after that, Cole wants to see you." A sadistic laugh erupts from her before she walks ahead of us. As we follow in her wake, I wonder how long she lasted under torture before turning – how many cuts, how many hits of the fist, how many truths. There's part of me that should feel sorry for her, but I don't – she doesn't feel sorry for me – and of all the people in the world, she should; she knows exactly what I'm going through.

"She really is a total bitch," I say. "And you got real strong" I say trying to smile. I need warmth. I need friendship.

"Small perks of my newest adventure," he says winking at me. I laugh. It feels foreign, but good. It's been a while. I lean back into him and try to weigh up the level of his loyalty, but it's hard in this place – the normal rules of engagement don't apply.

"Thank you," I whisper. I'm not even sure he hears me until I feel his kiss on my hair.

He lowers his voice to a whisper – he doesn't want Livvy to overhear him. "Addie, I know this is the worst time to ask, but I've just not had chance…"

"It's fine, Logan, whatever it is, just ask."

"Is Tyler okay?"

"Are you kidding me?" I ask, he stops at my words, and I'm staring him hard in the eye. He is still recoiling from the venom in my voice, and it's attracted Livvy's attention.

"Come on, you two love-birds, we haven't got all day."

"Coming!" Logan calls out after her, satisfying her that her wish is our command. He looks at me and shrugs, "Woah, Addie. What's the matter?"

"They haven't told you?" I whisper urgently. There's so little time.

He shakes his head, looking at me wearily, "Told me what?"

77

"Tyler is the reason all of this happened, Logan. He sold us out. He was working with Kaden. I don't know much, Xander wouldn't tell me everything. All I know is, Tyler was working with Kaden. He betrayed us all. He let the Shades in that night, and it was Tyler who handed me over to Kaden later. The only thing I know for sure is, he's gone and he won't be coming back. Xanders Elite saw to it.

"How?

"I don't have the details. I didn't want them, but he won't ever be back."

A mix of emotions play on his face; the shock and the hurt, anger and disappointment. He holds me a little tighter and rests his forehead against mine before he starts moving again.

"I'm so sorry, Addie. I can't even imagine… But I've got you Ads, you're safe for now. You should rest."

It's like a lullaby. I hear the words and my eyelids grow heavy, the lack of sleep catching up with me. I fight it but Logan makes me feel safe. I feel his arms lift me into the cradle of his chest, and his whispered words send me drifting into oblivion.

I wake to soft sheets under me and warmth wrapped around me. I open my swollen eyes and discover the warmth is Logan. He's wrapped himself around me protectively. He's watching me and I roll my eyes at him. I don't understand this shift.

"Creeper," I say with a smile.

"That's Mr. Creeper to you, thank you very much," he says making me laugh. He removes himself and a cold surge of air fills the space.

"So you're my new guard?" I ask him. I can't keep up with all of the changes here.

"Something like that. I think it was meant to be Liv... but Cole was worried to leave you two alone together for too long."

I snort incredulously, "Jeez, that's saying something considering he thinks Micah a perfectly safe option!"

"Micah is a socio-path, which means he's predictable. He wouldn't kill you, because he'd see that as a personal failing, whereas, Livvy... well, I guess I hadn't realized just how badly she was affected, how deep the hurt went, but well... you've seen. I think the girl we knew is still in there, deep, *deep* down. I just don't think she knows how to be her anymore," he says with a long sigh. The pain in his eyes is real; the love he felt for Liv is still there, but it's distorted by who she is now.

"We could bring her back you know..." the voice in my head says seductively.

79

"Ugh no! I thought you were gone!" I say.

"Sorry?" Logan asks, confusion colouring his cheeks.

"You're going to think I'm nuts. Well, more nuts…" I say hesitantly. I want to trust him, every cell in my body feels safe around him, but he's still one of them.

"How much do you know about what's happened to me since I got here?" I ask. I see the guilt wash over him.

"Too much," he admits. "I'm really sorry I couldn't stop it; that I couldn't save you, Addie."

"I guess that makes us even, huh?" I say with a twisted laugh. "So that means you know about her. The weirdo that is the other me?"

"I've heard rumours about it. That you burned up that asshole, Micah, real good. That you have power. More power than any one of us put together."

"Yeah, that's pretty much it. I don't know the extent of the power, but I seem to heal like a Fallen, I never would have made it this far if Cole wasn't my dad I guess. She's like a whole different person but part of me all at the same time. I think she's why Cole wants me." I sigh. "Why couldn't my parents just stay dead."

"Do you know who your mum is?"

"No, I don't know that I want to know. Micah says she was a demon whore, but who the hell really knows. If she was with Cole, she can't be anyone good – or sane, right?"

"I guess…," Logan says shrugging. His face crumples and he says sadly, "You know I have to take you to him soon? I'm meant to have only let you have a short rest before the healing bath, but you looked so peaceful. He'll be pissed that he's been made to wait."

"What the hell is a healing bath?"

"Exactly what it sounds like. I'm not sure what's in it, but it will heal you. All of your sores, your cuts, everything will heal fully. Your scars will fade to almost nothing."

"And the pain here?" I say pointing to my heart and then to my head.

Logan shrugs again.

"Bloody demon magic I assume?" I ask.

"Does it matter if it can make you feel better? I felt some of your pain. I've been trying to syphon it from you bit by bit, but I know I've barely touched the surface."

"You have? How do you even…"

"You probably don't want to know," he says, wincing a little.

"You're right. Lead the way."

"Oh, it's just through that door."

I walk into a bathroom. The tub is filled with a cloudy looking water. I did not expect something so normal and after everything I've been through, it makes me suspicious.

I strip the clothes from my body, trying not to focus on the pain of the movement, or from where my body has started to heal and where the clothing opens wounds. I slowly lower myself into the milky water and the relief is almost instant. *Mother of gods this feels like heaven.*

81

Demons might be asshats, but they know how to rock some healing power. I lay back and feel it as it starts to heal the wounds that cover my body, and my mind quiets a little in this moment of refuge. It takes a while before the feeling starts to ebb and I feel almost like myself again. I run my hands over my face and hair, wincing at the cuts there. I take a deep breath and sink below the water, submerging myself fully. I need to bottle this shit and take it home with me. I stay under for as long as I can manage before surfacing. I can feel the swelling in my eyes reduce, and the cuts on my lips and eyebrows heal shut. I feel like new.

Grabbing a towel from the nearby rail, I stand and get out of the tub. I dry off and see the colour of the tub has changed from a milky white to a rusty red. My blood. I shudder at the thought before pulling the plug and turning to the mirror. I can't believe it. I look like me – Hell, I look better than me. I freaking glow!

"Stop getting distracted, Addie. We need to find a way out of here." I hear her pipe up in my head again. *So much for quiet.*

"We're not going anywhere fast. Cool your shit. I want to know what he's up to first so we can stop it," I say quietly.

"We're going to regret staying. We could knock out the boy. He clearly cares for you, and we could escape."

"I will not hurt my friends!" I protest.

82

"Your weakness will get us killed. No-one is coming to save you. We need to rescue ourselves."

"Maybe so, but I will not hurt them. Not again. I already failed them once. It's my fault they're here like this." I hear a knock on the main door and tread quietly to the door to see who it is. I peak through the small space between the door and the frame. Livvy.

"Is she ready yet, Logan?"

"She's in the bath now. I'll bring her to you when she's done."

"Very well."

"What are you going to do to her, Liv? She's our friend. We need to help her get out of here." He pleads with her. I see her hand rear back and then hear the crack of flesh as she slaps him around the face. Shock roots me in place. The Livvy I knew would never hurt a fly.

"How dare you speak like that! She is the reason we are here, or have you forgotten that. She let us die. She let them take us. She was weak. We're going to help her fulfil her fate; make her all that she can be. We are the chosen, Logan. Do not let me hear you speak like that again." She spits at his feet before turning on her heel and storming out of the room. I sink to the floor, leaning against the wall. The Livvy I knew really is gone.

"Told you so," *she* says.

I need to go out there and talk to Logan. He must put himself first. He needs to survive this, too, but I can't make my legs work. I hear him pad across the room to the door. He pushes it open and slides down the wall next to me, drawing me close.

"I'm so sorry, Logan," I say, my voice catching in my throat as a sob works its way up. Thinking she was dead was one thing, but seeing what she has become kills another piece of my heart. I mourn the loss of my best friend all over again. Logan holds me close, saying nothing. I don't understand his loyalty to her. I mean, yes I know more than most how much he loved her – before... But that's not who she is anymore, she's not the girl he used to love.

"Come on, Addie, we need to get you to Cole. Keeping him waiting is never a good thing."

I nod, wiping the tears from my face and composing myself. I never thought I'd be this girl; the crazy hot mess. But here I am. I swallow it all down and lock it away inside. I have more important things to worry about right now.

Logan took me up to see Cole, but now Cole's gone and so are his personal demon hit squad. No-one is telling me anything, but from the tension I've picked up, something has happened. I was bought down to this god forsaken cell and left to my own devices. My guards, Thing One and Thing Two are back, standing stoically on the other side of the electric cell doors.

The voice in my head has been insistent since I was bought back down here. "If you let me out, we could be free."

The only problem is, I have no idea, not one, of how to tap into the power I feel thrumming under my skin, and last time I was sucked under, she took over. I don't want to lose control; I don't want to lose who I am. The voice quietens and I pace around the cell. I'm in a normal cell, not a torture chamber, so at least I can be grateful for that small mercy, but it's so goddamn cold down here! I guess it's getting on for winter now, and I'm thankful Logan pulled out a sweater for me.

I try not to focus on why Cole bought me here, and instead, sit down on the muddy floor wrapping my arms around myself. I close my eyes and picture myself away from here, sitting on a sandy beach, the wind whipping my hair around me. I can almost smell the salt water. Xander and Dimitri are wrestling in the water and Liv and Rose are sun bathing; laughing at Logan and Ty as they try, and fail, to play soccer on the sand. This is what life is like when I close my eyes. None of the bad things which have happened to me matter. Getting lost in my own fantasy, I don't notice when my cell door opens. Startled, I scramble to my feet. Looking up, I'm met with cold indigo eyes. I

have no idea who this guy is but he feels familiar to me –
something scratches at the edges of my mind, pushing me
to remember, but there's nothing. He stares at me silently,
as if he's waiting for me to react.

"Erm… Hi?" I say with a small finger wave. I have no
idea what to do right now. Who the hell is this guy?

"*You* are the chosen one…? I imagined you'd be…
taller," he says with a quirk of his lips. It's so quick I think I
might have imagined it.

"Hey!" I say.

"Now, girl, I am here to test you, and it is up to you
how much this hurts."

"W… what?" I stammer. I've had enough of being a
pin cushion.

His face is stern. "Be still, girl, and this won't hurt –
much." He strides towards me and places his hands on
either side of my head. At first, there's nothing, then I'm
screaming; falling to my knees as the images assault my
mind.

Xander a bloody mess, dying in front of me.

Dimitri lifeless on the floor of the Academy hall.

I scream at them to get up. They can't die. It's all over
if they die.

"This isn't real, Addie. Fight him," the voice says.

"I can't. What's the point? Look at them, they're
dead."

"No they're not! Snap out of it. Push him out. You just need to focus. Use me. Let me help you."

I try to push him away with my mind but it's no use; the grip he has on me is too strong. I can feel him trying to pull *her* to the surface. The feeling overcomes me and then I'm floating, watching myself from outside of myself again.

I watch my hands fly up and the stranger flies backward.

"You should not have done that, Scott Ashton. You know you are no match for us. Not once you let us out of this cage. You should be ashamed of yourself, Fallen."

He snarls at me... her... us... whatever. For a minute I think he's going to charge us, but then he seems to compose himself.

"One day soon, little girl, you are going to regret this! Once he has control of you, once he bends you to his will, you will be nothing but a mindless tool. And then, then I will make you know what it is to truly suffer. You'll be broken, and even your precious Xander won't be able to piece you back together. I'm not sure what will bring me more joy, breaking you, or watching Xander break seeing you that way. Finally, he'll feel some of the pain he caused me."

"We both know I cannot be broken. You can only control us for so long. He knows it, too. Why do you think he rushes to bring me forward, to unleash our power before she's able to control it? But once she accepts it, when she is able to accept what she is, she will be unstoppable," Aeveen says in a calm and serene voice. It's so trippy to watch myself from the outside. "She is more than any of you even know,"

"That demon bitch will be nothing but an empty husk. A whore for us to pass around," he says getting so close to me there is barely a gap between our bodies.

I see the slap coming before there's any time to react. The crack is hard as his hand connects with my face, then everything goes dark. *Son of a bitch!* I jump forward, and the feeling of my fist connecting with his nose brings me more pleasure than I care to admit. I hear the delicious crunch of bone before blood bursts satisfactorily from his face. Having control of myself again is revitalizing.

"You bitch! You'll pay for that!" He lifts his hand to me again when Thing One steps forward and lifts him out of the cell.

"That's enough for now, Scott. Master will not be pleased to hear you struck her," he says, scolding that dickhead. Scott sulks off down the corridor and even the pain in my hand isn't enough to wipe the smile from my face. Damn that felt good. I look up and see Thing One smiling at me and I smile back. Maybe today won't be such a bad day after all.

I've spent the last few days focusing on tapping into Aeveen. I need to learn how to merge with her, and she's not shut up about it since that douche-canoe bashed me about. It's hard to get past the fact there's a whole other person inside of me. I have no idea who she is or why she's there, and it's not like people here are exactly talkative.

Since Cole seems to have disappeared with his lieutenants, I've been left alone, which has been a nice change of pace. I've been fed and watered, and I discovered Thing One and Two are actually Brock and Aaron. They're Fallen, too, but other than the occasional few words, they don't really speak much. I'm not sure if they're keeping me in or keeping everyone else out. I've not seen Liv or Logan.

When I sleep I try to go back to the clearing where I found Rose, but I've had no luck. I don't seem to be able to dream when I sleep. Aeveen says its due to a charm on the cell I'm in; she can feel them. It's a containment charm, meaning the magic within the cell is dimmed. Nothing comes in, and nothing goes out, which also dampens the chance of me being able to get out of here, even if I do manage to merge with her.

I've been so focused on all of this that I've managed to lock most thoughts of Xander away in a box deep inside my head. Every time I think of him, I miss him so much it hurts. I also start to think on how he might get me out of here. I'm quick to quash those thoughts and I remind myself that I'm more than capable of saving myself. I think back to the me of a year ago, before all of this. That me would be horrified I was leaning on a man to get me through everything. One thing I've learnt from everything is that I can be strong on my own – that doesn't mean I can't cry, or lean on other people; I've learnt that isn't weakness, it's just part of being human, but I can still handle the hard stuff. Like the fact that I thought two of my best friends were dead, turns out one is actually just a raging bitch.

"Are you ever going to shut up and actually work at this?" She says.

It sucks I can't shut her up.

"The feeling is mutual, believe me. Do you know how ridiculous your thoughts can be? I've put up with it for YEARS!"

Okay, I can do this. I sit down on the dirty floor and close my eyes, picturing myself in a meadow. I see my double standing in front of me, except, it's not me; her face is devoid of all emotion, like the lights are on but nobody's home.

"Are you ready, Adelaide?" Aeveen asks, her voice emotionless and monotone.

"Ready as I'll ever be. How exactly am I meant to do this?" I question.

"Like I explained before, you need to reach out to me. You've seen me as a physical being, but you need to be able to feel for me, feel the power inside you and then hold on to it."

I sigh. I have no idea how to do this. She sits down in front of me mirroring my posture, and puts her hands out in front of her like she's a mime. I raise my hands and press them to hers. All I feel is her icy cold hands, I feel no spark.

"You need to reach for it, Adelaide. We're connected, you'll find it."

I take a deep breath and try to stamp down the frustration. I'd like to hit her, but I'm not sure what hitting her would do for me right now, I'd probably just end up hurting myself. *Awesome*. I close my eyes again and concentrate on the icy feeling of her hands, imagining a cord from my centre, traveling up through me, down my arms and through my hands into her.

"That's it, Adelaide, keep pushing!"

I manage to stretch the cord up her arms but as I try to reach her core, I feel the cord snap back into me. God Dammit!

"You're getting closer, Adelaide. It has only been a few days."

"I know! But you're inside of me for crying out loud! This should be easier. None of this makes any sense!"

"We were separated when you were an infant, Adelaide. I assume it was done to mask what you truly are and to ensure you were not executed. What you are is not something that would be accepted in your world."

"What do you mean?" I ask. *How is it she knows all of this and I have no idea?*

"What we are, what we *will* be, is something which has never been. It has only ever been spoken of in whispers. Seers long ago spoke of someone like us, but it has been long forgotten. If people find out what you really are, you will have bigger things to worry about than falling in love with some Vampyr, or the fact that your old best friend is a… what did you say, raging bitch."

"What exactly am I?"

"You are part Fallen and part something else – something not human, Adelaide. No matter how much you hope you are."

"What! Of course I'm human!"

"No you're not, but that's not what's important right now. Right now, you need to focus on reaching your power, otherwise you're going to have much bigger problems than you could have ever imagined."

COLE

"Aeveen, is that you?" I ask. I've been waiting patiently for Micah to reach her again, and this is the first time she's broken through since Addie took control back.

"What do you want, *Father*." She emphasizes the last word. I wonder how much she knows of the truth.

"I just want to speak to you, Aeveen. I want to explain the truth about everything; make you understand I'm not your enemy."

"Oh really? Is that why I'm locked up in here? Why you torture the body I live in?"

"I'm doing this *for* you, Aeveen, don't you see? Without this, you cannot be free. The more I torture her, the more you can come through, the weaker she is, the stronger you become," I say.

She seems to think this over before asking, "Why would you do this?"

"Because *you're* my daughter, and I don't think it's right you should be the one to suffer while Adelaide gets to live your life. You should have been as one, but your mother bound the part of her that is you; she made it so you would be trapped. I don't want that for you: I want you to be free, for you to be by my side."

"Why would my mother do that? Why would you let her?"

93

"Your mother feared you; and I did not *let* her – she hid you from me. I didn't even know of your existence until very recently, Aeveen; that is when I began my search for you. The joy of knowing I had a daughter; an heir! Then I found out what she had done to you and I made it my mission to free you so you can live your life fully. It is your turn, is it not?"

"It would be nice to live fully, but what about Addie?"

"Addie is the one who kept you submerged. It is because of her, you've been locked away. Why would you care about her?"

"Because she is part of me. Why can we not merge?"

"Because, my darling, Addie does not want to merge with you. She's selfish and wants to keep her body for herself. She's as bad as her mother, wanting to keep you locked away. But you're the powerful one, Aeveen. When you remember who you are you'll know that."

"And what do you gain by freeing me?" she asks. She's definitely observant, I'll give her that. Even if it is frustrating as hell.

"I gain a daughter; someone to share my life with - someone to rule with. I gain a power in my arsenal. I'm not going to lie to you, Aeveen, I will never do that, but I cannot say the same for others. Look in Addie's memory, you'll see I never lied to her, not like the other people around her. With you awakened, I would have an unstoppable force on my side and no-one would dare to try and put us down again."

"So you wish to use me, Father?"

She's sharp, and I feel a sense of pride. "Never, Aeveen. I'd never make you do anything you didn't want to do, but if you choose to align with me, there are steps we need to take before we can be truly free. Do you trust me?"

"I do not understand this trust... but you have a logical and reasonable explanation, and I can tell you are telling me the truth. What do you need from me, Father?"

"I need you to fight. Fight Addie with everything you have. I need you to push her down and take control. I will help you in every way I can. Will you do that, Aeveen?"

"I will try my best, Father. Addie is starting to fight me again. I can feel her in the back of my mind."

"That's okay, let her back for now. We have a lifetime."

"Thank you for saving me, Father."

"I would do anything for you, Aeveen," I say before she fades away and the body of Addie slumps forward. The relief I feel is overwhelming; knowing I managed to reach Aeveen and bring her to my side. Now we have a fighting chance. Elation floods me in my success.

"Micah, keep going, we're close, I can feel it. Bring her back to me," I say before leaving the room and letting him get back to work.

It's not long now until Xander Bane feels the pain he caused me.

XANDER

Rose insisted on speaking to Addie again before we left, but she's not been able to reach her. I'm trying not to dwell on what that could mean. For now, I'm focusing on the next steps to get her back; to have her in my arms.

First things first, Kaden. Rose has rounded up two experienced transporters to take us directly to him, and the itch of impatience under my skin is becoming too much. I've felt helpless too often recently. This, visiting Kaden, is something I can do. Something I have to do to get to her.

I see them approach and try to relax. Every single muscle in my body is taut, completely on edge. I don't think I'll truly relax until I know Addie is safe.

"Are you all ready to go?" Rose asks.

I can't help the scowl that appears on my face. We've been ready to go for what feels like forever. "Yes, we're just waiting on you, Princess," I bark out. I don't have it in me to feel sorry for the harshness in my voice. "Let's go."

I take the hand of the transporter closest to me and close my eyes. I feel the air shift around me, and embrace the feeling of falling. What feels like minutes, but in reality is a few seconds later, I feel solid ground beneath my feet and the swirling air calms to a light breeze. I open my eyes and look around me, making sure everyone else made it okay. Benny is bent over in a rose bush, so I'm guessing it's his first time. Dimitri looks a little pale. Other than that, our small party seems to be fine.

"Thank you for assisting us," I say to the transporters before they return to their home.

I start towards the front door of the monstrosity standing before me. It looks like someone in the Old World had far more money than sense and tried to create the hideous love child of a castle and a stately home. The gothic towers, gargoyles that decorate the top of the walls, and wooden beams on show are exactly Kaden's style. He always loved the human's penchant for tacky horror. The lion head knocker on the front door dominates it. I lift it and slam it back down three times. Seconds pass before the door is opened by a tall female red-head.

"Well, well, well, if it isn't the long lost brother and his merry band. What the hell do you want?" she asks.

"I need to speak to Kaden," I say.

"Well no-shit, Captain Obvious. I mean, what do you want? Kaden's busy," the red-head snarks

Rose bursts forward and hugs her, squealing with delight, "Celeste! I've missed you."

"Hey, little bird, what brings you here. Where's the mouthy one?"

"That's why we're here," I say, interrupting.

The look of disdain on her face lets me know how she feels about me and I couldn't give less fucks.

"Addie is missing," Rose whispers.

"What the hell! Why didn't you say so? Get in here. Kaden!" she yells and it echoes around the hall. With our special hearing it doesn't take much to get our attention, I'll be surprised if Kaden's ears aren't ringing after that – mine sure as shit are.

"What the hell are you yelling for?"

I hear Kaden before I see him. He strolls down the oversized staircase that takes up most of the entrance hall, with another Fallen following closely behind him.

"Michael!" Rose squeals running towards the blue haired Fallen. She meets him as he gets to the bottom of the staircase and jumps into his arms. It seems strange to me that she would greet the people who were once her captors in such a way, but I guess it was technically Kaden who was her captor; she eyes him warily.

"Big brother! What brings your grumpy arse to my humble abode?" Kaden asks as he saunters towards me,

99

arms open greeting the whole group, stopping just a few feet in front of me with Celeste to his left, and Michael (with Rose still tucked under his arm) to Kaden's right.

"I need your help," I say, straight to the point. I don't want to be here asking anything of him and I'd rather get it done and out of the way as quickly as possible.

He barks out a laugh, and there's a mischievous sparkle in his eye. "I never thought the day would come, brother. What, pray tell, could you possibly need my help with?"

I look him straight in the eye and I see him stiffen slightly when he sees how serious I am.

"Addie has been taken. No-one has any solid leads on where exactly she is, but whispers tell us Cole has her."

Kaden swears enough to make a sailor blush before turning his anger at me. "Can you keep nothing safe, Xander? I gave her back to you in order to keep her safe, and out of his clutches. I should have fucking kept her! I should have known you wouldn't have the balls to do what was needed to keep her safe!" The emotion pours from him. I guess Addie really did affect him when she was here. Michael clasps his shoulder and seems to plant him in place.

"Calm yourself, Kaden," he says. The bass of his voice is so low I swear I feel the vibrations in my chest. He turns towards me. "When was she taken?"

"About three and a half months ago. We were unaware of her disappearance until two months a month and a half ago. We were away on a mission," I say. The shame burns my throat.

"Are you bloody kidding me! She's been gone that long and you're only just coming to us? I thought you loved her, brother. Do you have any idea what he could have done to her in that time?" Kaden yells at me.

"I am all too aware, Kaden. Now calm yourself so we can find her. I'm here now and I'm asking for help. We have managed to reach her, well, Rose here did, but she has no idea where she is. All we know is it's bad and we need to get to her as soon as we can. Do you know where he is?"

"We do, but it's not like we can just waltz up to his front door and take her home, Xander. He lives in wolf territory," Kaden says before letting out another string of cuss words.

"Which pack?" I ask. *Please don't be the Shadow pack. I can't stand them; an egotistical bunch of bastards who get caught up in their own hype.*

"It's Kas Narayana's land. Up in what used to be Canada."

Well thank god for that.

"It's still not going to be easy though, Xander. Kas is still pissed at you after the last time you were there," he remarks with a grimace.

101

The last time we were there, Kas' Beta, Clay had got out of line before completely flipping his lid and killing two humans. We had to put him down but it caused a rift; Kas felt it was none of our business, the Fae felt differently.

"Yeah well, let's hope his new Beta isn't such a raging douche. Clay wasn't exactly the sharpest tool in the toolbox," I say with a smirk. Kaden laughs a little before looking around at us all.

Kaden and I haven't seen eye to eye in a long time but he's my brother, and I'm beginning to realise he actually cares about Addie, regardless of what he'll admit. I'm not sure how I feel about that exactly, but there is nothing I can do about it right now; I have bigger things to worry about.

"Can you get in touch with Kas? Let him know we're coming for a visit and that it's not a social call, but to keep it quiet. The last thing we need is someone in Cole's camp to hear about our presence there."

"I can do that," Kaden says. He turns to Michael and issues instruction. "Michael, make sure everyone who needs a room has one. Get them food. You know the drill."

"Of course," Michael says with a nod of his head. He turns to us and smiles. "If you will all follow me."

ROSE

Michael leads everyone to their rooms before taking me to the room Addie and I shared in the past. He ushers me in and wraps me up in the biggest bear hug.

"I've missed you, sweet pea," he says into my hair before kissing the top of my head. "I only wish we weren't together under such horrific circumstances."

I nod before stepping back from him and sitting on the bed. "It feels like forever since we were here. I can't believe it was only, what? Nine months?"

"I know baby-girl, and now our Addie has gone and gotten herself into a whole world of trouble all over again," he says perching next to me.

"I can't believe all of this. I thought after everything that happened, we'd finally get some sort of normalcy. We deserve it. But when I spoke to her, Michael, oh God, the things they've put her through," I sob.

"How exactly did you speak to her, Rose?" he asks, looking confused.

"That's right, I forgot you guys didn't know I'm a Dream Walker," I blurt out quickly. It's not like it's a secret, but I wasn't exactly offering up information about myself before I met Addie. The shock on his face is about what I expected.

"A Dream Walker? But you were here for so long, and with that monster for all that time before you came to us. Why didn't you use it to escape, or be rescued?" he asks, his disbelief apparent. I understand it, I'd react the same. I shudder thinking about everything that happened before.

"I didn't know how to use it – not until Addie. She helped me work at it. We'd go to sleep in here and talk in our dreams, scheme about how to get out of here. I've not been able to connect to anyone else, but I can always reach her, no matter the distance. Only I… I haven't been able to reach her the past few days, Michael," I whisper. "I'm so afraid for her. What she's going through is more than any person should have to live through. What if she finally gives up? I don't know anyone who could survive that."

"Don't you worry that pretty little head of yours, doll. Addie is the strongest person I know; stubborn and sassy as hell too. I bet she's driving them crazy. She'll get through this, and she'll be okay," he says before hugging me tightly again.

A knock on the door makes me look up, and Kaden's head pops around the door. I sit up a littler straighter, old habits die hard.

"Michael, I need you. We've got some shit to sort here before we leave to head north," he says before disappearing as quickly as he appeared.

Michael sighs before squeezing me again, then he's standing and a wave of disappointment roils over me. I had hoped for more time with him.

"Duty calls," he says. "We'll get her back, you'll see. You should get some sleep; I have a feeling it's going to be a long few days."

XANDER

I run my hand through my hair, it's a wonder I'm not bald. Advantages of being damned I suppose. I'm surprised everything today went as smoothly as it did. I think if I'd been here for any other reason, I'd have had the door slammed in my face.

The urge to storm in and try and take control of Kaden's people is overwhelming. Leaving the details to him is completely out of my nature, but it's his contacts we're using, and considering mine and Kas' history, I'd probably end up being more of a hindrance than a help. Dimitri opens the door and I can see immediately that the worry is starting to take a toll on him. The guilt for the situation we're in slams home again.

"Xander, stop it. Your guilt is written all over your face. There's nothing you could have done, and now we're doing everything we can. You need to build your strength up and prepare for what's to come." He throws me a blood-bag, the liquid inside has been warmed. I bite into it

105

and silently thank him; blood is horrific when it's cold. I finish quickly and he throws me another.

"I can't remember the last time you fed; I knew you'd be hungry." He shrugs when I throw him a questioning look. I hadn't realised he paid such close attention. "Do we have a plan for when we get to the Narayama territory?" Dimitri asks.

"Not yet. I'm waiting to hear from Kaden to make sure we're even welcome. Not that that will stop me going, but it will change the tactics of the entire mission." *There is not one thing of this earth, above or below, that will stop me getting to her.*

A sharp knock at the door announces another visitor and Dimitri answers it while I change my shirt.

"No need to strip off for me, handsome. I can see all of your deliciousness even with your clothes on."

I turn to see Michael stood in the door way looking me over like I'm his next meal. *I don't even know what to say to that.*

"Don't worry, dear boy, I don't bite. Well, not unless you ask nicely." He winks at me and I can't hold in the laughter that bubbles up inside. Dimitri's laughs follow my own. This guy is outrageous. "At least I know how to inflate my ego when Addie bashes it to nothing."

"She does have a habit of doing that, doesn't she?" He states with a sad smile on his face.

"We'll get her back. From what I've seen, Kaden's just as invested as we are in getting her back."

"I'm not worried about that, I know we'll get her back. I'm just worried as to what will be left of her when we finally get there."

I walk up to him and grasp his shoulder. "Addie is one of the strongest and most stubborn people I have met in my entire existence. I'm almost more worried about her driving Cole so insane that he gives up his mission and just kills her to stop her shooting her mouth off."

He smiles a small smile. "I said something similar not too long ago. However, Rose is fragile; I'm not sure she should come with us."

"Believe me, my friend, I tried, but you try telling her, 'No'." He laughs again, this time full bodied, rather than vacant and sad. The twinkle is back in his eyes.

"Addie was a bad influence on her." He smiles. "Speaking of which, Kaden wants us in the war room. He has got ahold of Kas."

CRASH

Chapter Eight

ADDIE

Micah is back, and I'm not sure how much longer I can stay conscious. His love for knife work is obvious through his attentions today. I'm amazed I've not passed out purely from blood loss... Though that could be something to do with the fact I'm part Fallen.

"Come on, sweetheart. You know what you need to do. Unleash your inner demon and you'll be free!' He squeals in delight as he sees the shock on my face. *Demon?*

"Oh that's right. Daddy dearest didn't tell you, did he? Your mother was a demon whore, one who would do anything for her next fix. Just rotten, wretched filth!" He spits. "You're no better, are you, sweetheart? Just a filthy little whore! You just like to play hard to get. I know you want to give it up and hand yourself over to me. I bet that inner demon whore of yours is begging to get out, too. This will all stop if you just let her out to play."

I stay silent with my head bowed; my thoughts whirring at his latest revelation. I can't be part demon, can I? Pain slams through me as he rips my head backwards by my hair and puts his blade against my stretched throat. It stings as he slowly slices through the thin layers of skin. The cut feels so shallow, almost like a paper cut, but it's enough for tears to spring in my eyes. I try to blink them back. I will not let him see me cry. Not ever. Even though I know I'm starting to break, I can feel the fissures splitting my soul, I will never let him see it. I close my eyes and take deep breaths. He takes the blade away and the cold metal is replaced by his warm breaths. My eyes shoot open when I feel his tongue run along the cut he just made on my skin. The shudder that runs through me, is impossible to stop; the feeling of violation overwhelming. I buck against his touch, trying to push him away from me.

"You're disgusting," I spit at him. A crazy smile graces his face.

"I try my best, sweetheart," he says before licking me again. "It really is so much fun, especially when someone is as tasty as you."

I scream, my frustration and desperation rising to the surface.

"That's it, princess. Let it out, let it all go." He smirks. He's winning and he knows it. God damn it! I feel the holes in my soul grow bigger, and I feel myself slipping before the world turns dark.

ROSE

"I'm going to try and reach her again, Benny. There's no point in trying to talk me out of it. I'm so worried about her. I just need to know she's still alive."

"Rose, this is a bad idea. What if you can't reach her? What then? I don't want to see you go further down; I hate it when you're sad." He draws me in close. He's so much taller than me that I feel fully cocooned when I'm in his arms. He's like my very own safe harbour during a dark storm threatening to destroy everything.

"I love that you want to protect me from this, Benny, I really do, but we both know if the situations were reversed, Addie would run through fire to make sure I was okay. I can't let her down. I know I'm not equipped to help her the way the rest of you are, but this is something I can do that no one else can. I need to do my bit."

He sighs, his resolve weakening. I know he can't really stop me, but I hate it when he's mad at me. He leans down and kisses me gently, causing the butterflies to whir in my stomach – just like they did the first time he kissed me and every time since.

"Fine, I don't like it, but I understand. She's my friend, too. It kills me that I can't help her. Just, be careful, Rose.

We both know that if anything happens to you in there," he pauses to plant a kiss my forehead, "it happens to you out here, too."

"I'll be careful, I promise," I whisper, pulling him close. He lays me down on the bed beside him and I look at him, questioning his move.

He smiles. "If you think I'm leaving your side, sweetheart," he says.

I roll my eyes and tuck myself into his side. "Fine," I say, "Just try not to distract me," I tease. The shocked look on his innocent face makes me laugh out loud.

"I have no idea what you could possibly mean."

I slap his chest playfully before getting comfortable and closing my eyes. I build the scene in my head, like last time; the pretty meadow, with walls of energy that only Addie can pass through, before reaching out to her mind. I don't know *how* I'm connected to her, I just am. I picture the bright white string that runs between us and slowly pull on it, bringing her to me. I try to squash the excitement rising in me; I can feel her on the other end. The relief that she's still alive floods through me.

That's when I feel her pain screaming through our connection. It rips through me as if I'm her. I feel every cut and burn, every tear and bruise. I can't help but scream out, I try to hold on to her, to let her know I'm here, but her pain overwhelms everything. The connection snaps throwing me backwards. I open my eyes to see Benny stood over me yelling my name. Each breath I take feels like fire ripping through my lungs. I try to speak but I can't find my voice. Tears run down my face as the pain takes over. I can feel the warmth of my own blood as it trickles down my hand, out of my mouth, eyes, nose and ears, and I know that my own body has been harmed in the same way as Addie's. There's too much to focus on. Benny picks me up in his arms and hurries me out of the room. He's running with me, yelling out for help. I try to keep my eyes open, but they feel so heavy. I see Kaden and Xander above me as I'm placed onto another bed. Numbness spreads over my body and I feel myself relax; the pain leaving me.

Whoever would have thought that being numb could be such bliss?

I hear voices. *God, they're so loud. Why can't they just be quiet?* I try to open my eyes but my eyelids feel so heavy. I manage to open them a little but soon close them; *It's so damn bright!* When I try to speak, it feels like I've swallowed sand. *Why the hell does it feel as if I've drank more tequila than my body weight?* I ache everywhere.

That's when it hits me. *Addie. Oh, Addie*. I can't help the sob rising or the tears falling. The voices quiet and hands are on me.

"Come on, Rose. Wake up, please!" Benny pleads. His hand squeezes mine, but it's hard to reciprocate – I don't know that I've ever felt this weak in my life. "That's it baby," he says. "Please open your eyes."

"Too bright," I manage to whisper. There's movement and then the light dims. I try again to open my eyes but they feel as if someone has glued my eyelids together. Peeling them apart, I see Benny looking down at me. The worry is etched on his face.

"How are you feeling, doll face?" Michael asks. He's sat at the end of my bed.

"I feel like I just did ten rounds with one of the Elite goons," I say, making Michael giggle. Benny's not so amused and he frowns. "Don't look at me with that tone of voice Mr. I'll be fine. Where are the others? Have they found Addie?" I ask.

They both answer me with their silence. I push myself into a sitting position with a groan.

"We need to find her. Technically, I'm not hurt, but she will be. I only connected with her for a minute and I feel like an elephant just sat on me."

Michael chews on his bottom lip. He's not got good news. "Once you passed out and we got you here, Xander and Kaden holed themselves in the war room to hash things out. So far, there's been shouting and smashing, but I'm not sure much progress has been made."

"Why aren't you with them? Where is Dimitri? Those two can't be expected to play happy families and get their shit together by themselves."

"They asked us to leave," Michael replies, looking more than a little unhappy.

"And you listened to them? Are you out of your bloody mind?" I ask exasperated. "This is going to get us nowhere. Take me to them." I give them both a pointed stare. At this rate, nothing is going to get done.

"Rose, you need to rest. We don't know how badly all this will have affected you. It's so rare that it happens. You need to wait until a healer arrives to check you over," Benny says matter of fact, his hand pushing my shoulder back down onto the bed.

"Benny, if you think you can keep me in this bed then you're wrong. Now, you can either come with me, or you can find something else to do, but I am going to talk to those thick-headed brothers. Even if they do terrify me. My best friend needs me and I'll be damned if I'm just going to lie here while she suffers. I am not asking you, I'm telling you. Take. Me. To. Her!"

I rise from the bed slowly. *God, I feel awful.* Michael is beside me in a second to help steady me. I smile at him in thanks and then see the flash of a scowl directed in Benny's direction. *What's that about?* I don't have time to process that dynamic right now so I tuck it away for later when I'll extract more info from Benny.

"Come on sweetie. I'll take you to them now. God knows this is going to be entertaining even if nothing else!" Michael says, wrapping his arm around my waist to help me walk out of the room.

Benny stubbornly stays behind.

We walk through corridors to what Michael calls the war room. *Thank God it's on this level!* I don't think I could have managed stairs, and after all of that crazy back there, I would have hated to ask Michael to carry me. I hear the raised voices long before we reach the closed doors. He knocks sharply before entering. I'm pretty sure the mess in here is a direct result of leaving the brothers alone. They're in opposite corners of the room, the wooden table in the middle of the room is split down the middle and books are strewn across the room with their pages torn out. Pictures that once adorned the walls are now scattered across the floor; the broken glass around them.

"For crying out loud! What the hell is going on in here? Look at this mess. What on earth have you been doing? Because it sure doesn't look like you've been working towards finding Addie!" I shout. "You should both be ashamed of yourselves!"

They have the decency to look ashamed of their actions, each looking like a scolded little boy.

"He started it," Kaden says, pouting.

116

"Really? That's your response. Mature!" Xander says rolling his eyes and crossing his arms over his chest.

"Don't you start with me, big brother; this is entirely your fault. If you had been man enough to keep her safe, loved her enough to put her first, we wouldn't be in this bloody situation!" Kaden yells. Michael flinches beside me. I guess this is why he and Dimitri left without too much of an argument.

"Don't you dare!" Xander roars. "You have no idea the things I have done for her. The things I have sacrificed to keep her safe. If it wasn't for you, Cole wouldn't have been able to get to her in the first place. Don't even presume to think I do not love her. You have no idea."

The tension is this room is stifling, and if Addie didn't mean so much to me, I'd probably run out of here and let these two work through their issues in private.

"Hey!" I say, probably louder than necessary, but they seem to have forgotten I'm even in the room. "Do you really think this is the best time to hash out who's better than who? Or who loves her more? Really? Surely we have more important things to focus on – like bringing her back to us. All of this is pointless if she dies," I say. The word 'dies' has jolted me and it's the same for the brothers, but I haven't finished. There's this new strength channelling through me.

"I felt what she's going through, for less than a minute, and I was out cold. Do you really think it's more

117

important to go through all of this, when that's what she's going through for hours on end? We need to pull together and help her. That's what's important," I say, softer this time. I let go of Michael and walk over to Xander, placing my hand on his bicep, encouraging him to look at me rather than the floor.

"I know you're hurting right now, and I know you're busy blaming yourself for everything, too, but do you really think she'd want to see you like this?" I say before turning my attention to Kaden. "And you – do you not think you owe it to her to get her out of that hell? I know you have an evil streak Kaden – I can account for that more than most here – but I know that's not all you are." Emotion flickers in his eyes it's guilt mixed with…

I don't want to think on what it looks like. That's another thing to think about later.

Chapter Nine

XANDER

It took two days to finalize the details - the downside of letting most of the worlds technologies die and needing to be covert, but we're finally on the road heading towards Narayama territory. We're driving because it's less noticeable than a group of Fallen flying with Fae and human passengers. I have no doubt Cole has scouts looking out for any kind of movement. I'm travelling with Dimitri, Rose and Benny. The black Range Rover screams luxury. Something I don't feel I deserve, but this is what Kaden has so this is what we get. The fear in my chest slices through me again; the thought of life without her makes it hard to breathe. I grip the door handle, my knuckles turning white while I try to compose myself.

Dimitri is in the driver's seat and he looks over to me – questions on the tip of his tongue, which he keeps to himself. I'm grateful for his silence. My friend has known me a long time. I daresay he is one of few who knows how badly this is affecting me. I have fought in many wars, lost friends, been injured myself, but none of this compares to the emotions tearing me up. Knowing Cole has Addie and it's my fault is almost unbearable. If I hadn't left, if I'd have just contacted her while I was away, I would have known sooner; she could have been spared, but I let my sense of duty to her mother, and the protection of our world come first. I will never let anything come between us again, if only I get her back.

The car is quiet as we eat the miles on the I94 towards what used to be Toronto. It's less than a day's drive from Kaden's house in Old Chicago. We drive through the night to avoid coming across anyone else who might be travelling; there are many Vampyrs and Fae with cars, nowhere near as many as the humans used to have, but enough that we could be anyone. I watch the world go by out of the window, anxious to reach our destination and finally feel like I'm doing something to bring her back to me. There is no version of my life without her. She is everything. I just regret I realised it too late, all I can do is hope that she will forgive me and give me another chance.

I look into the back of the car and see Rose and Benny are both sleeping and I should try to rest, but I haven't slept properly in months. I don't need as much sleep being Fallen, but I know I won't be at my strongest if I don't get some soon.

"Xander, she's going to be okay," Dimitri says quietly, not wanting to disturb the others. "She can handle this – whatever it is. I know Addie; she'll survive if for no other reason than she won't let him win.

I'm right there with you, but you know…" he hesitates, knowing his about to say something I'm not going to want to hear. "You really need to get over whatever is still between you and Kaden. Especially since things with Kas are probably going to be tense too. You need Kaden on your side."

I say nothing. I know he's right – of course he is. Addie is more important. I rest my head against the head rest and close my eyes. We'll be there in a few hours, and I need to build myself up for whatever is coming, but I'm plagued by the fact I need my brother's help, and after everything that has happened, I don't know if I can trust him. It all happened so long ago that even to me, some of the details are foggy now.

We had fallen along with our sister, Kaden's twin, Elaihn. She was sought after by many, her beauty unmatched by another. Her tall waif frame, topped with the longest golden hair, and eyes that shimmered like the sea on a sunny day. She and Kaden took after mother, whereas I looked almost exactly like my father – or so everyone said.

Others had already Fallen, and many more were still coming. We, like so few others, had been lucky enough to survive the end of life as we once knew it. Our paradise had been destroyed and so many had perished. The wars between our people had been our downfall. Egos running riot; our home, Addatria, consumed by the chaos. Addatria was dying, and there was no way to save it. It had been taken by those who thought they should claim our piece of the world. The rebels had risen up and tried to shackle and control us.

We stayed together, the three of us alone, our parents and so many of our friends had passed. Kaden and I were lucky to survive considering our positions back home. I might not have made it out if not for Kaden pleading with me – for Elaihn's sake. And so we fell, leaving our home to its fate.

Our sister was strong, one of the fiercest woman I have ever known - other than our mother. Female warriors were almost unheard of in our world, but my mother was a force to be reckoned with, and she had taught Elaihn to be the same. Only, with Elaihn's fierceness came a great gentleness. She could make even the darkest day shine as bright as the sun, but if you angered her, she could ruin *your world and burn it to the ground. After the death of our parents, she lost herself. She was so very broken.*

Once we fell, we sought out old friends, and came across our General, Cole. We stayed with him. He had fallen before us, escaping early with the intention of building a safe place for those of us who survived. While we had watched Earth our entire lives, we had never entered the domain of the Fae. Everything was fine for a time, but then our kind started dying and no-one knew why. We were meant to live for a long time. We were not immortal as the Fae were, but we had a much longer lifetime than the humans. Yet here on Earth, we were dying.

Cole had become something of a father figure to the three of us, he took us into the home he had built, helped us create new lives, and everything was starting to look up until Elaihn became sick. Kaden was a mess, refusing to leave her side, leaving it to Cole and I to try and find a cure. We scoured the earth looking for something to help my sister, then we came across Queen Eolande who offered us a solution; something that would help all of our kind. We sent for Kaden and Elaihn. Bringing her such a distance was dangerous, but the alternative was unthinkable.

Queen Eolande struck a deal with Cole – she would help all of our kind, giving each of the Fallen an elixir of immortality, and in return, we would help to protect the Fae and the humans. Cole had to ensure none of our kind caused any harm to either the Fae or the humans; harm would be punishable and the nature of that punishment decided by the Fae. Cole agreed and the elixir was created using the blood of a royal. The Fallen would be granted immortal life. And so, the process started. There were not many of us left, maybe two hundred in total, left from thousands. We called them from all over the world to us, and began administering the elixir. Kaden and Elaihn arrived with some of the last, and Elaihn was in a bad way, but the Queen saved her, along with the rest of our kind.

With Cole as our new leader, as per his agreement with the Queen, he called upon the thirteen lieutenants he had left, Kaden and I each being one, and created the hierarchy system that would rule our kind, creating thirteen houses. We were each allocated vital roles in rebuilding our civilization while helping to keep the Fae world secret from the humans.

Many months passed before the blood lust began. It gripped so many, so quickly, but luckily no humans were injured. We ran many human hospitals and collected as many blood bags as we could to look after our people. We had it under control, or so we thought.

Elaihn was out on a raid one evening with Kaden and his house. Against my advice, they were helping to keep the Demons at bay, to ensure the human race did not find out about anything 'other'. She had never fully recovered from the death of our parents and she was unstable, but she was still one of the fiercest warriors we had, and so they went. Demons had been causing havoc with the humans who lived in our city. The mission went well; the situation was handled and they were on their way home when Elaihn flipped. The adrenaline from the fight mixed with a vicious wave of blood lust turned her. She killed many of Kaden's team before attacking a human. Kaden managed to wrestle her from the human, who escaped, before knocking her out and bringing her home.

Then the Outbreak happened and the Fae knew it was down to Elaihn. The very thing that kept us alive, the pathogen which replenished us, was killing the humans. She was taken to the Fae court; her punishment was death. It was the tipping point for our kind. Kaden was distraught and I buried my own pain to comfort him – but his grief took him beyond my reach, and so he fell in with Cole and the others who felt they had been betrayed by the Fae, that we had been lied to.

Although Queen Eolande had not known the elixir would cause the blood lust, many did not believe her, and so the lines were drawn as the humans died in the thousands. The contagion, which spread from Elaihn, ravaged the Earth and so many souls were taken. The only survivors were The Immune, but Earth as we had known it was destroyed. Just as our home had been. I lost my sister, my brother, and Cole all in one day; the pain of it was unbearable, and I swore to myself in that moment I would never let anyone get close again. I pushed it down and stood my ground against Kaden and Cole. I knew Queen Eolande. I had been there when the deal had been struck. I knew she had not lied to us, so I could not side against her, pitting me against the only family I had left, casting me as a traitor in their eyes.

And so, the war began.

I open my eyes and daylight is breaking through the darkness. The pink and purples paint the sky. The contrast is vivid against the black of the night. I hear the crunch of gravel under our tires and know we're nearly here. The road cuts through the woods, leading us to the main reservation. The sun tries to break through the canopy of the trees above us.

When we drive through the clearing, I'm impressed at how far this reservation has come since I was here last. A large building sits in the centre of the reservation, towering above the other buildings. After the war, Kas rebuilt this place in a likeness to what it was before. He felt the wolves needed the comforts of the old world in this new one. The wolves were here long before us, though not quite as long as the Fae. Many houses are scattered around and what looks like a medical centre has been built to the left of the main building. We pull up in front of it, the others pulling up behind us before exiting their cars. Kaden finds me and pulls me to one side.

"I'm sorry, brother," he says, clasping my shoulder. "I know this wasn't your fault, but I can't help being reminded of Elaihn. This whole situation, it just… It's a lot, you know?"

I pull him into a hug. "No, I'm sorry, Kaden. I hadn't even considered… I've been so preoccupied. I hadn't thought about her much, I haven't really since, well since Addie. not until today at least."

"You forgot her?" Kaden shouts and I take a step back; my hands up in front of me.

"Of course not, I couldn't. I just mean that I haven't been plagued with memories of her the way I used to be. The guilt over her death doesn't haunt me so much anymore. I learnt to forgive myself for everything that happened. She wouldn't have wanted any of this."

"They're a lot alike," he says avoiding my eyes. "I don't want to go through that again."

"I guess they are," I agree. "Do you think that we could try, for Addie's sake, to work together on this? I need you, brother. I don't think I can do this without you."

He looks up at me, and the guilt he feels shines in his eyes, though I'm not sure why. "Of course, Xander. I'd do anything for her – and for you."

I nod before making our way back to the group. As we reach them, I see Dimitri talking to a pretty dark haired woman. Two young boys are chasing each other in circles. Their laughter is so young and so innocent. For a minute, getting lost in how happy they seem lightens the darkness surrounding me. The innocence and naivety of children, oh to have that again. I'm approaching them, Kaden just a step behind me, when Kas walks out of the main building. The boy I once knew has grown into a man. It's not a surprise he's still Alpha. Standing at about six foot four, he's hard to miss. The entire party are drawn to him, his raw magnetism backed up by his broad shoulders and thick arms. I have no doubt if Addie were here she'd be commenting on how dreamy she found him. His long dark hair, which reaches down to his chest whips around him in the wind. I smile at the thought of her meeting Kas. She has always wanted to meet a wolf. I recall the night she had peppered me with incessant questions about them, we were talking about some of the missions I'd done in the past. It is a sweet memory but it only makes the pain worse when I come back to the present.

Kas' look is calculating. He never was a major fan of the Fallen, or our Vampyrs, and now we're littered across his territory. When his eyes fall behind me to Kaden, Kas' steely glare softens and a warm smile spreads across his face. "Kaden, my friend! How good to see you!" He says walking towards us and embracing Kaden.

"I just wish it were for other reasons," Kaden says.

"You and me both, you and me both," he says before turning to me. "Xander, I hope this visit goes better than your last."

"It couldn't go much worse," I say, trying to lighten the mood.

A small smile appears on his face. "That much is true. I say, let the past be the past. We have more important things to worry about, hey?" he says putting his arm out to me in truce. I clasp his forearm and we shake on it.

"I'd like that very much, old friend."

"Then it is done. Now come on in, I imagine you are all tired. This is my sister Dani," he says pointing towards the dark-haired woman I saw Dimitri talking to earlier. "She will make sure you all have everything you need."

The girl blushes and looks to the floor before muttering an agreement. A shy wolf? Well, that's a first! She says hello to us all, and Dimitri seems enraptured by her.

Kas leads Kaden and I into the main hall leaving Dani and Dimitri talking, before taking us up a flight of stairs to a large open room. "We have plenty of guest rooms on this floor. We'll use this room as a dining hall. I've already sent scouts out to the house we think Cole is holed up in.

They've been gone a day, so I expect them back shortly. Do you need anything else? I want to check in with Jackson. We announced your arrival last night, as you can imagine, some of the pack weren't exactly jumping for joy, but once I explained it was for the Reborn, they got on board."

"The Reborn? You mean she really is?" I ask.

He nods. "I spoke to her, only once a week or so ago. She did not say much, but the fact I could speak to her is enough to convince me. You know I can only speak to those with the wolf affinity."

I'm stunned. I knew it was a possibility but having it confirmed. Well shit!

"Wait, what?" Kaden asks, confusion colours his features. I forgot he doesn't know.

"I'm surprised Cole never told you," I say. "Though he always did keep his cards close to his chest. Let's get everyone else here so I only have to go through this once?"

Kas hollers for Dani and asks her to bring everyone in. Dimitri, Michael and Celeste head up the group, followed by Benny and Rose, then the rest of my Elite. Most come to the front, separating themselves from the wolves, but Dimitri hangs back with Dani. I'd pay more attention to that if I had time; it's about time he had some fun, but for now I have more pressing things to worry about. A few wolves, who I recognize, walk behind them, including Jackson, Kas' Beta. Kas stands at the front of the room as everyone sits in front of him. Kaden and I stand either side of Kas showing a united front to both sides.

"Sorry to keep you folks," Kas announces. "But before we get started, we feel it necessary to make sure you are all aware of all of the facts surrounding Adelaide, and everything at stake."

Kas steps back, nodding in my direction. The floor is mine. I can feel the wave of guarded hostility from the pack. "I know many of you are going to have questions but please try to keep them until I finish. I'm sorry I have kept this from you, but until now, it was for your own sake, and Addie's. I'm not sure where it's best to start from, so I'll start from the beginning." I go on to tell them the story of Queen Eolande and the secret she shared with me; of my role in this history of Addie. I can see they have a million questions – and doubts to go with them, but I need them to believe. "I have watched over her for many years, ensuring no harm came to her, and I was successful in my duties… until recently."

There are murmurs from those in front of us. Kaden's eyes widen as he begins to understand the implications of what I'm saying. "It wasn't until a few weeks ago that I understood why Addie was the target for Cole's ideals. He is her father."

The room erupts with shouts and gasps. Kas steps forward, drawing the attention of the room.

"Adelaide is the Reborn," Kas declares. "The one the prophecy speaks of. This is why we must ensure we get her back. We cannot let her fall into the wrong hands. I'm sure, had we all been aware of this before now, we would not be in the position we're in." Kas stops to side-eye me. So much for let bygones be bygones. "But we're here now, and so we must deal with it."

"What prophecy? I've never heard of the Reborn?" Rose asks from the back of the crowd. I look to Kas; the Fae and the wolves are The Keepers of the Histories. It is rare for a Fae not to know, but considering her life so far, it is not shocking.

"The prophecy was spoken long ago, towards the end of The Dark War. It speaks of the one who will have the power to tip the balance; one made of air and earth, both evil and pure – with more power than any other who walks the Earth. The Reborn will have the power to bring an end to life as we know it, and tip the scales.

It was not said in who's favour this tipping will be, but the fact Cole knows what she is, and has her, is enough reason for us to be afraid. If his plans succeed, the world could be a much darker place. We all know how long it took for the world to heal after the war. If he rallies her to his side and awakens the power within her, he will be unstoppable," Kas tells the room.

132

Quiet descends across the room; so quiet it's as if no breath is taken. The shock in the room is rife as the weight of truth settles on each of us. I look towards Kaden and he looks like he might break. He notices me looking at him and composes himself; that unemotional mask slamming back down.

"I'm sure many of you have questions, but I'm sure you'll understand and agree that getting Addie back from Cole is our first priority. I need to go and meet the scouting party I sent out yesterday, I urge you to get settled, there are more than enough rooms here for you all. Eat, rest, and prepare yourselves for what is to come."

DIMITRI

I watch everyone reel from the information. The shock is palpable, and undercurrents of anger and fear run alongside it. I get why people are angry; I know that I sure as hell was when I found out. I look down at Dani, Kas' sister, who has attached herself to my arm. She's so small, I just want to wrap her up and protect her from the world, and that feeling scares me. I don't let myself get attached to people, especially wolves, and especially so quickly, but there is something about her that calls to the most primal parts of me. I can't seem to escape it. I'm not sure that I even want to. I'm not sure which part scares me most.

"It'll be okay Dani. We're not going to let it get that far, we just needed everyone to be aware of the potential things that could go wrong if we don't all work together," I gently say. She looks like a deer caught in the headlights, her eyes wide and doe-like.

"I know," she says. "I mean, Kas already explained most of this to me so I wouldn't freak out in public; I'm just scared for my boys. They've already been through so much in their very short lives. I don't want them to suffer any more. Not if I can help it."

"Don't you worry your pretty little head, darling. We'll keep you safe," I reassure her.

"Like I haven't heard that before," she says before quickly covering her mouth. She looks at me apologetically. "Sorry, I didn't mean it like that. I just… never mind, I'm just sorry."

I look at her and realise there's a lot more to her I don't know yet, but I want to. There's sorrow in the depths of her eyes, a hidden hurt; such great pain. I want to know what happened to her. She's so quiet and withdrawn. I noticed it when we first got here. She looks like she wants to fade away into the background and have no-one notice her, but I noticed her. When she looked at me, it was like I was struck by lightning. Rooted to the spot, transfixed by her.

"It's alright, darling. You don't know me yet, but you'll see. I keep my word."

"I guess we'll have to see about that won't we. Please excuse me, I need to get back to my boys. I left them with the girl next door while came here. I don't like leaving them for long."

"Sure thing, sweetheart. I'll be seeing you," I say, watching her walk away from me. As much as I hate to see her go, I've got to say. The view watching her leave is real nice.

"Found a pretty little thing to distract yourself with, sweet cheeks," Michael says as he stands next to me and following my eyes.

"Don't even start. She's not like that," I say with an unexpected fierceness. The protectiveness I feel towards her already is unreal. I need to get a grip on myself.

"Woah there, cowboy. No harm meant. I just meant she's cute." He shrugs.

"Sorry, I just. I don't even know," I say, running my hand down my face.

"It's always the best ones who hit us the hardest, and when we least expect it," he says with a mischievous glint in his eye. "I've got my eye on you two, cupcake."

"Yeah, yeah. We're not here for that. We're here for more important things than me getting some tail," I say, trying to shrug off whatever the hell is happening to me.

"Ahhh, don't try and fight it, cowboy. It's when you struggle that you fall faster. You'll see." He laughs before he sashays over to Celeste before following Kaden out of the room. I look back in the direction Dani headed. *It's not too stalkerish if I make sure she gets back okay. Right?*

KADEN

The conflicting emotions rage inside – not that you'd know to look at me. I learned a long time ago to hide anything real. This whole thing has been one damned mess up after another, right from the very start.

I knew when Cole came to me in the beginning, this was a bad idea, but my stupid petty feelings toward Xander won out – and I ended up hurting Addie. The moment I saw her in the clearing, I knew I was doing wrong, but there was too much at stake for me to turn back, and so I took her. Then I got to know her, and I knew I couldn't hand her over to Cole.

I did everything in my power to keep her safe, but she ended up with him anyway. I cut almost all ties with Cole after I sent Addie back to my brother, believing it to be the best way of keeping her safe. I even tried to bargain with him to give me her friends. I should have known that wouldn't be the end of it. Especially, when he wouldn't give them up. But I never imagined she was his daughter. That *she* was the one spoken of so long ago.

I remember right after the war, when Cole was still licking his wounds from his loss, the prophecy was spoken. His obsession with finding and controlling the chosen one was tantamount to nothing. It coveted his every thought, day and night. I dismissed his obsession, having never put much stock in prophecy. Now, I wish I'd paid more attention to his plans.

Back then, I was too busy hating my brother, hating the Fae for what they had made me. My own vengeance blinded me for centuries; hate fed my actions and depravity became a way of life. I fed the underbelly of the underworld, catering to the wishes of Demons, dark elves, and the Fae who had abandoned their normal way of life. I made a name for myself as the one who could cater for any need you could dream up – for a fee of course.

Regret courses through my veins as I think about how my actions directly bought us to this moment. Shame fills me as I leave the room. Everyone is still talking about the revelation. I make my way to one of the empty rooms, shut the door and lean against it.

I'm not sure when things changed. I know it started when I took her, but the more time I spent with Addie, the less appealing the other stuff became. The themed nights at the mansion for all of those paying for their deepest and most horrific desires, the things I sought out to ensure my clients were pleased, all of this stopped after I saw her reaction to it. The look on her face when she saw what was happening around her, chipped away at my black, un-beating heart. The more time I spent with her, the more I realized there was no way I was handing her over to Cole.

And after that night, when everyone was messing around, singing karaoke, relaxing as if there was no divide, that's when I knew I had to tell her the truth.

I knew it played right into Cole's hands, but I wanted her angry at Xander. I wanted her to trust me, and when she put her hands in my wings, fuck me. I almost fell to my knees, willing to give her the world. At the time, I had no problem with feeling the way I do towards her, but now, with the chance of having my brother back, I know I can't feel this way.

But I don't know how to stop it.

I push my hands through my hair and pull on it, begging the pain to take over the tornado in my mind. I need to get her back. I need her to be okay, and I won't stop until she is back. I will set the world on fire to make sure she is safe. But, knowing once she's here, I'll have to watch her walk off into the sunset with my brother… I don't know how I'm going to deal with that. I don't know how to see them together and not feel the raging jealousy that already bubbles up within me. Knowing that she doesn't have a clue. She would never feel for me what she does for my brother – and it kills me more than it should.

A knock on the door slams me back to reality. I pull myself together and put on a mask of indifference, ready to face the world. I open the door and find Michael and Celeste stood in front of me. I step back, allowing them into the room and close the door behind them. They are the only two people in the world with whom I can truly be myself. Each of us at our lowest point, drawn together by pain and tragedy. Family, born from the worst things life could throw at us. I would give them everything they desire if I had the power to do so. They've both been through so much, both before they met me and with me.

"Can you believe this?" Michael asks, stunned. From the look of Celeste, I'd say she feels the same.

"I had no idea. I found out at the same time you did. If I'd known, I would never…"

"We know you wouldn't have, Kaden," Celeste says trying to comfort me. "Even if no-one else believes it, we know. What are we going to do?"

"Whatever we need to. We can't let him have her. She deserves more. She's worth… everything." The words leave me before I can stop them. Neither of them are oblivious to how I feel, but this is the first time the words have been said aloud.

"We will get her, Kaden. Even if it costs us, she will be safe."

"Safe. And back with my brother," I say unable to conceal the bitterness in my voice.

XANDER

"Xander!" I turn at the sound of my name being yelled behind me and see Rose running towards me.

"Xander, wait!" I stop and let her catch up. When she reaches me, she bends over at the waist, sucking in breath.

"Man, I need to work our more," she says, standing upright.

"Can I help you, Rose?" I ask.

"Actually, I think I can help you. I think I can get you into Addie's dream. I'm not sure how long I'll be able to do it for, but it's got to be worth a try right?" she says in a stream.

I swear she doesn't take a breath. This news is amazing, but I don't want to get my hopes up. "Really? What makes you think you can do this? Why couldn't we do this before?"

"I didn't know it was possible before. I've been researching some of the scrolls father gave to me, and it says that it has been done in the past. I'm willing to try it if you are."

"Of course I'm willing to try; I just don't want anyone to get hurt, Rose. I know how hard these things can be on you."

"I'll be fine. I just figure it's not fair I'm the only one that's been able to see her. But maybe we shouldn't tell Benny just yet." She giggles nervously.

"Thank you, Rose. Thank you so much. Have you been able to reach her since last time?"

"No, I haven't," she says looking down and fiddling with a button on her top. "But I won't stop trying. I'm not saying this will work, I have no idea. I've never even connected with anyone but Addie, but I need to do something, and if this can help, then I'm all for it," she says with a quiet passion.

"Okay, when are you proposing we do this?"

"Tonight? Dimitri should probably be there, but we'll have to keep everyone else away."

"Agreed. Okay, I'll send Dimiti for you at about nine and we shall try. If you can't do this, Rose, it doesn't reflect on you. We all know how bad you want Addie back."

"Thank you, Xander, I appreciate it. I'll see you later."

I pace my room while I wait for Dimitri to come back with Rose. I hope to hell this works. I know that some people don't understand what we have, or why we're together, but it doesn't have to make sense to them. They don't know what she means to me, and I really couldn't give less of a shit what they think. All that matters, is that it makes sense to us. I just hope I get my Addie back. I'd sacrifice everything, even myself, to save her from everything that she's going through.

141

A knock sounds at the door and I rush to open it before waving Dimitri and Rose in. Hope floods through me, I might actually be able to see her; tell her everything I should have said before I left for that stupid recon mission. I should have just stayed home and put her first. If I get her back, I'll spend the rest of our lives putting her first.

"Are you ready?" Rose asks. I can see the hesitance in her. She's nervous, and I don't blame her. This isn't a small thing to attempt. Even for someone like her.

"Ready as I'll ever be. Where do you need me?"

"Lie down on the bed and get comfortable. I don't exactly know how the Fallen sleep or dream, but I'm assuming it's the same as the rest of us, so it shouldn't be too hard."

I nod and follow her instructions. She climbs on the bed beside me and takes my hand in hers. I can tell how tense she is.

"Everything will be fine, Rose. Even if we can't reach her. Relax."

She lets out a long breath and settles beside me, closing her eyes. I'm not sure how much time passes, but when Rose enters my mind I become very aware. I look around at where we are, it's a small field in a forest, protected by a bubble of light.

"Rose, this is incredible. Is this normally where you see her?"

"Yes, Addie actually dreamt it, so I figured it was a safe place in her mind, I just recreated it so she can come back."

"Amazing. How do we reach her from here?"

"I need to connect with her, but I put the bubble in place so that no-one else can enter. I've not been able to connect with her for a while, so I don't know if we'll manage it tonight, but I need to try."

"Okay, what do you need me to do?"

"I just need you to be quiet so I can focus on her," she says before sitting down crossed legged and closing her eyes. I sit in front of her and do the same, taking her hands.

"Maybe I can help? I just need to focus on thoughts of her right? Maybe I can help amplify your thoughts?"

"It can't hurt," she says.

I close my eyes and focus all thoughts on Addie; of her as a child, discovering the world we live in, aged twelve, getting her first kiss from a boy and then punching him for being gross. I chuckle a little remembering that one. Then I focus on her now. I picture her face when Michael and Celeste bought her back to me. Her hair whipping behind her in the wind, strands covering her face, and those eyes. Her eyes pierced through me, carving up my heart, destroying me for anyone else. I knew in that moment she would only ever be mine.

"Xander?" I hear her voice, and I think I'm imagining it. I open my eyes and look around the bubble. I see her, stuck outside.

"Addie? Is it really you?" I rush to my feet and towards her, she flickers in and out, like an old TV screen. "Addie don't go!"

"Xander. Oh my god Xander I miss you so much!" I see tears run down her cheeks and it kills me.

"Rose, why is she outside?" I shout.

"I don't know," she says fearfully.

"Addie, you need to come in here. I can't help you out there."

"I can't, I can't get through," she says before falling to the ground.

"I'm coming for you, sweetheart. I won't be long. Nothing on Earth can keep us apart."

"Save me, Xander. I don't know how long I can keep her back. The demon inside me, she fights me every day, and they help her. They want her, not me. I'm dying, Xander, I can feel it."

"You're not a demon, Addie. I don't care what they've said, how they've poisoned your mind. I need you to hear me."

"You don't know who I really am," she sobs. It breaks me to see her like this. To know it's my fault for not being honest with her before.

"Addie, more than anyone else on this plane or any other, I know exactly who you are, and baby, you are not a demon! Your mother is far from a Demon. Don't let them win, Addie." I put my hand up to the light and she places her hand on the other side and I swear I can feel her. She starts to flicker in and out and I try to push through the barrier to get to her.

"Addie!" I shout.

"I love you Xander. Always." I hear her whisper before she disappears fully from sight.

"No!" I yell. I turn to Rose, the desperation fuelling my anger. "Bring her back! I can't let her go like that. I had more I needed to say to her!"

"I can't, Xander, I don't know what happened, or why she couldn't get through. I feel so drained. I need to take us back."

"Dammit, Rose, please. Just try!"

"I'm sorry, Xander," She says before disappearing from sight too, then I'm surrounded by darkness and I swear I can hear laughing in the distance. Cruel and evil, sending shivers down my spine.

I'm shook awake and open my eyes to see Dimitri stood over me with a very pissed off Benny knelt down by Rose.

"Rose, we need to go back," I plead.

"Hell no!" Benny roars. "She shouldn't have done this in the first place, it could have killed her! I told her not to even mention it. God dammit Rose!"

"You saw her?" Dimitri asks quietly and I nod.

"Yes, briefly. She's so broken D. I don't know how much longer we have before it's too late. We need to get her back. Now."

Chapter Ten

ADDIE

Life is made up of moments. Defining moments. Forgettable moments. But they all build up together, until one day they crest and you have to deal with the result. The fallout. I think back across the events of my rather extraordinary life and wonder how I ended up here. I try to pinpoint the moment everything took a turn for the worst; the moment I made a decision that led me to be where I am, but I can't for the life of me recall it. You'd think it would be a pinnacle moment I couldn't possibly forget, and yet, I think it must have been one of those ordinary, everyday forgettable moments. Maybe that's why my punishment has been so unrelenting. To lose everyone around me I cared about, and finally, to lose myself.

I don't know how much longer I can survive the punishments. My body can't take much more, and I'm at the point of losing hope.

Other than my brief and blissful moments with Xander last night, I've seen no one but Micah for days. His torture is unrelenting. Each day, I've lost more of myself, and I can feel Aeveen getting stronger. Each day, I feel her surge forward, and my hold on her slips before she takes over and pushes me down. Fighting her for control exhausts me mentally. I'm not even sure why I'm holding on anymore, except for the fact I'm too stubborn to let go. I'm not ready to give in. I hear Aeveen's ramblings continuously, driving me insane. How she's 'so much stronger' than I am. Her 'purpose is greater' than mine. That she 'needs to be let free'. She spoke to Cole last time she broke through, except that time it was different. I couldn't hear or see, it was as if I was floating in darkness void of everything. There was nothing but my own thoughts, and it was terrifying, not knowing if I'd ever be me again.

Since then, she has changed. Her hunger to be let free is more intense, and she fights me day and night, torturing me from inside while Micah ravages me. She wants to be with Cole, she only calls him 'Father', and if I even think badly of him, pain erupts inside my head making my nose and ears bleed. I'm so glad I got one last chance to see Xander. I wasn't lying when I told him last night that I'm dying. I can feel Aeveen's presence growing and I fear she's going to overwhelm me soon. I've learnt I can heal quicker than I ever imagined, and because of this, I can be hurt more than I ever thought possible. Each time, I think of Xander and try to go to a happy place, she wails inside my head and I can't shut her off unless I am asleep – at least there she doesn't torture me. I sag forward in my restraints.

I'm lost.

Micah's sadistic giggle starts again, followed by a slow clap. I look up and see Cole stood in the doorway.

"Well done, Micah my boy! I think you might have broken the filly," he says with a delighted smile on his face. *Asshole!* I think. The pain rips through me making me scream out. My back arches against the retrains, my body fighting itself.

"Ah, and it's good to see Aeveen doing her part, too. Soon we will be together again, my daughter, we will be all we were meant to be and no-one will be able to stop us."

I hear him through the pain and that's when I feel the last thread of control snap. The pain breaks me and I float into the darkness. *At least it doesn't hurt here.*

AEVEEN

I open my eyes. I have finally won. I'm free, and I can't hear her in my mind either. After my talk with Father, I had to break free and help him take vengeance against those who trapped me. He told me the truth; about how the Fae and the Vampyrs worked together to imprison me. To lock me inside of this body so that I could never be free. They thought me too dangerous to roam the Earth without even giving me a chance. He asked me to fight for him, fight for myself against the many who fought to keep us weak. After my initial refusal for making Addie, and in turn me, suffer, he explained that he did it for me. That it was the only way he knew to set me free. He told me merging with her wasn't going to work, that I'd lose myself to her, and she'd gain my power. It didn't seem fair; she'd already been able to live. It was my turn. So I fought.

I'm still in the wretched chair, but I see Father kneeling in front of me.

"Aeveen, my darling, well done! You did it. You're finally free."

"Hello, Father." I turn to Micah and smile. "Thank you, Micah for your assistance. Now can someone please unbind me?"

"Of course, of course," Father says. "We'll get you cleaned up and show you to your room. Only the best for my daughter. I am so proud of you," he says. I can see his pleasure shining through. A warmth fills me – it feels foreign. I think I'm happy he's proud of me. Emotion is going to take some getting used to. He unties me and pulls me in close, hugging me. I stiffen; I've never been hugged before, and while I have Addie's memories of such a gesture, it is strange to be embraced.

I stand still until he steps back from me.

"It is okay, Aeveen, we have a lifetime for you to adjust. Let's go upstairs and get you settled. Olivia will be around if you need anything."

I nod in response and follow him away from my place of captivity to my new freedom.

Once upstairs, he leads me to what he calls my room. I look around, searching Addie's memories for what these things are. Opulence is the word. Everything in the room is shiny. The walls white with gold features and trimmings, which match the bed. It's made of white wood with gold engravings. The knowledge floods through me and I take in her memories and filter the emotions out. I don't want to feel the way she did. I don't want to be influenced by her. I want the chance to be my own person. I frown slightly as I look around at it all.

"Is everything okay, Aeveen?" Father asks.

"Of course, it is just a lot to take in all at once. I'm trying to learn so much, but also keep her buried. The task is tiring."

"I should have known. I'm sorry, darling. I'll call Olivia in to help you in any way you need."

"Thank you, Father."

"I will leave you for now. Come and find me when you're ready and we'll eat. I can answer any questions you may have over dinner," he says before turning on his heel and leaving the room. I feel... overwhelmed. There is so

151

much... everything. Working through it all is going to be hard.

The door opens and Olivia enters.

"Addie?" she asks, looking me over wearily.

"No," I respond. "My name is Aeveen. Though I believe you knew this body as Addie."

She looks me up and down warily. "You could say that. Cole sent me to take care of you. I'll be your guide for a time."

"Thank you," I say. "Maybe, in time, we might be friends."

She is shocked by my words. I imagine it might be hard to be my friend considering her past with Addie, but I don't know many people in this world and it would be nice to have a friend. She composes herself and smiles at me before walking into the bathroom.

"Get undressed while I run you a healing bath," she says. "Once you're clean, I will take you to Cole."

"Okay, Olivia." I say peeling off the dirty, blood-stained clothing. I know I should be repulsed by it, and that I should feel pain from the injuries of this body, but I feel nothing. I know I should connect more, but I do not believe this would be wise. Addie made foolish mistakes because she was ruled by her emotions. I do not want to be a foolish girl. I want to please Father, so for now, I will stay detached and keep myself removed from emotion.

Livvy

I can't believe she's not Addie even if the eyes are a dead giveaway, they're freaking *red!* But it's still so strange Addie's gone. Even after everything, I miss her. That doesn't matter anymore though. Finally, we can go forward. I don't know everything Cole has planned, but I know all of this was crucial to move forward. I wince a little, thinking about how Logan is going to react when he finds out what has happened.

After their last meeting, Logan was forbidden from seeing Addie again; Cole suspected Logan was losing loyalty. I know I need to look out for myself here. I have to fight each and every day not to be weak. The weakest link is expendable, and I don't want to be expendable ever again – that's how I ended up in this mess.

I've learned so much since I turned, from the fall and how the outbreak began, to how they learn to change the immune to build their ranks. I've made myself a crucial part of Cole's team by learning everything I can about our history. I'm not about to lose that. Not even for Addie. I know if she knew everything I had suffered through, she would forgive me everything. I have no choice but to fight for survival – even thrive – in this new world.

Once the healing bath is ready, I help Aeveen into it. The damage to her body is extensive, I'm amazed they survived. It is so hard to separate one from the other in my mind. I scald myself, *Addie is gone. Aeveen is here now. Just do as you must. Kindness is weakness, you learnt that the hard way.*

"Olivia?" she asks, hearing my full name in her voice makes me feel like I'm in trouble.

"Please, call me Livvy."

"Okay, Livvy. What is it like out there?"

"In the house?" I question, confused by her line of enquiry.

"No, out in the world. I have not had a chance to experience outside; all I have is the knowledge from Addie's memories, but I want to form my own opinions."

We sit and talk about the world while she lies in the bath with her eyes closed. I relax and lean back against the counter as we talk. It almost feels like the old days and I'm beginning to understand why Cole offered me this chance. It's like a blank slate with her, the chance to have a friend, the new me and the new her. He asked me to befriend her, to make her feel comfortable, in doing so, he gave me this, too. Everyone thinks he's awful, but they don't see this side of him. They don't know that he only does what he feels is right, that he will do whatever it takes to avenge those who need it.

COLE

At last, everything is falling into place. As I walk through the halls, ensuring everyone is doing their part to secure our success, I cannot help the grin spreading across my face. It is a shame I lost Kaden from the cause, but I have gained many others who have been, and will continue to be, vital to my success. Aeveen is one of the last puzzle pieces.

I reach my office and shut the door behind me, thinking back over everything that bought us to this moment. I call down and ask for food to be bought to my office for Aeveen and I. I don't want to overwhelm her, but I want to mould her to my way of thinking. I need her to stay on my side. She is the one to tip the balance; she will end the rule of the Fae once and for all, and I shall be King, like I always should have been. I deserve to rule. I have sacrificed everything for this.

I started it all by pushing Elaihn over the edge. I thought her death would cause the Fallen to overthrow the reign of the Fae. I hadn't counted on Xanders sense of duty, or the loyalty he'd inspire in others.

He is the reason I have been outcast; condemned to this hell. For centuries, I have been plotting my revenge, to take away everything he believes in. Using Kaden's anger towards his brother was one of my more brilliant moments, but I hadn't counted on the girl changing him. The chair beneath my hands splits. And Addie, she was so much stronger than I could have imagined; it took far too long to break her – but my plans have evolved.

Anger washes over me but I draw it back. Anger isn't needed right now. Now I have to focus on preparing Aeveen for the fight to come. I have big plans for her, and I'm counting on Xanders heroics. I underestimated him once before but I won't make that mistake again. I know how swayed he is by his heart, and I intend to use it and destroy it. To destroy him.

"Cole?" Olivia is at the door with Aeveen. I smile at them both before waving them in.

"Come in please. Make yourselves comfortable. I've sent for some food. Olivia, you're welcome to join us."

Olivia nods and settles herself down.

"Aeveen," I say, smiling warmly, "I've asked for some heated blood to be bought up for you, too. Though I'm not sure if you need it."

"I do not believe Adelaide ever drank blood."

"No, she didn't, but she also didn't have your power. Please, drink it. The last thing I want is for you to get sick."

She looks unsure, glancing at Olivia for guidance. She nods slightly. She's smart and she knows that this support won't go unrewarded.

"If you wish," Aeveen responds. I see they bonded already in their short time together. Good, I can use that.

156

Olivia is power hungry, and cut throat. She will ensure Aeveen is ready. A knock on the door signals our food and two boys bring it in and lay it out on the table before leaving.

Aeveen slowly picks up the goblet of blood and brings it to her lips before sipping. She is so hard to read, I cannot tell what she is thinking or feeling; I do not like it. She takes a further mouthful of the blood before drinking down the rest of the glass in one go.

"Good girl. Thank you. I am sure that it will be useful to you when we start training with your powers."

"I do not think I need much training with my powers. They are all I have ever known," she replies.

I hide my annoyance at her speaking back to me. Olivia winces with Aeveen's brazen insubordination.

"Even so," I say smiling tightly, "we will begin training in the morning. I would like to see what you can do."

She still gives me nothing, her face devoid of any expression. "Why?" she asks.

"I'm sorry?" I say, tightening my jaw.

"Why do we need to train? Why do you need to see what I can do?"

"As I explained before, Aeveen, you are a fundamental player in my plan to defeat those who cast me out, the same people who trapped you inside of Addie. They imprisoned you, the same way they did me. It is justice to do the same to them, if not worse. They should

157

be punished for their behaviour and must be stopped from attempting it again."

She chews my words over and I think, *this might be harder than I first expected.*

Chapter Eleven

XANDER

The news about Addie and her heritage went down about as well as I had expected. What I hadn't expected was Kaden's reaction. Not many will have noticed, but I know my brother, even if we haven't been close for so long. I hadn't thought about how he might feel about Addie, and just thinking he might care for her causes an immeasurable pang of jealousy to shoot through me. I try not to think about it too much as I deal with the questions I'm asked once Kas and Kaden have left the room. I answered those I could before I retreated to one of the empty rooms. I needed to gather my thoughts and prepare myself for what is to come.

We've already been here a week, and time is flying by without much actually happening. I lie on the bed with a weight on my heart. I will love Addie until the last breath leaves my body, and the thought of her loving another person cripples me. All week I have been trying to rein in my thoughts, but my imagination runs wild. I can't escape the image of her being with my brother rather than me. I try to push it down into the same box I hide everything else, but that box is close to breaking point.

I pull myself up and leave the building. I need to distract myself with something, anything. I find Kas outside with a group of wolves who are training. They fight differently to us, most chose to fight in their wolf form; they are harder to hurt that way, faster and more agile. They're much bigger than normal wolves, and their pelts range in colour, but it's the eyes that give them away; they shine so bright. To see them is to know they are something more. Some of the more powerful ones like Kas, can control their change. Right now, his teeth and claws are extended and his eyes swirl like fire, but his body is still that of a man. I watch from the side lines as he spars with Jackson, his Beta, who is also in his part-wolf form. It has been a long time since I fought with the wolves, but their power and aggression is immeasurable. They are some of the most brutal fighters I have ever come across, more so than most Demons. They are unforgiving by nature, stubborn and headstrong. Its why I was so surprised at Kasabian's easy forgiveness.

I watch them for a while, then Kas brings it to an end. He turns to me and grins with his extended teeth baring. "Xander, old friend. Many of my wolves have not fought

160

your kind. Care to help me Demonstrate our differences?" he challenges. There is no way in hell I'm backing down from this.

"I'm sure my brother would love to help out, Kas," Kaden shouts as he steps beside me. "Anyone want to take me on, too? I could use a decent fight." He smiles a cocky smile, his head tipped as he challenges the wolves. I can't help matching his smile.

"Of course I'll help you Demonstrate, Kas. I'll show your wolves what a real warrior looks like." I laugh at the growl he sends my way.

"The Bane brothers always did talk a big game. We'll see if you can back it up, old man. Jackson, you will spar with Kaden. Let's show the pack what they're in for."

The crowd around us grows, both of wolves and Fallen. Kaden and I strip off our tops. We might not need our wings, but there's a reason we fight this way. No limitations, no restrictions. I crack my neck, tipping my head from side to side while Kaden jumps up and down on the spot getting his blood pumping. I get the feeling he needs this as much as I do. I step forward getting in to position to fight Kas.

"You sure you're up for this, old man?" Kas taunts as he darts from side to side, watching my every movement like the hunter that he is.

"You wish I was an old man Kas, that way your defeat could be said to be a sympathetic loss. Letting me win. Let's see what you've got."

He darts forward and catches me on the jaw with a strong left hook. His paws are like shovels! I stumble a little before finding my feet. I hear cheering from the wolves around us and Kaden chuckling from the side line.

"That one was free. The next one you'll pay for."

We spar. Kas has learnt some new moves since the last time we did this so I don't come away scot free, but then neither does he. After we draw it to a close, stopping Kaden and Jackson from killing each other. We eat before going to Kas' office in order to go through the intelligence his scouts have gathered. Now, I find myself sat here, head in my hands listening to Kaden and Jackson bicker about what is the best next step. I have no idea what is in their past, but if they can't put it behind them, I'm going to smash their heads together!

"Kaden! Jackson! Please, that is enough. I have had enough of your back and forth, if you cannot put whatever it is between you aside, I will ask you to leave," I say, reaching my point of tolerance. The both quieten down and retreat to opposite corners like sullen children.

"We need to have a look for ourselves," Kaden mumbles from his corner.

"I think you're right," Kas agrees. "We can't agree a way forward without seeing it for ourselves. Let the three of us leave in an hour. Jackson will continue the training of the wolves, and I will make sure Dani caters for your group."

"Thank you, Kas. Kaden, let's go clean up and change," I say turning towards Kaden before gesturing for the door.

Dimitri approaches me after Kas and Kaden have left. I can already tell I've got another fight coming.

"You can't think I'm going to stay behind, Xander. I'm not leaving you with them for a start. I still don't trust either of them, but it's not just that – this is Addie. I've watched that girl since she was ten years old. That's eight years of being there for her, being her friend, watching out for her, picking her up when she's been knocked down, both literally and figuratively. You can't expect me to just sit back and watch as everyone else does all they can to find her."

"I get it D, if our roles were reversed I'd feel just as justified as you are in your point, but right now, I need you here. I know you don't trust them, but there's so much at stake. Michael and Celeste will be here, so will Jackson. I need you here to make sure the proverbial shit doesn't hit the fan. I also need someone to be able to keep Rose and Benny in line. I swear that girl is becoming more and more like Addie each day. I am only leaving you here out of necessity Dimitri. I would much rather have you by my side."

"I do not like this, Xander – not at all. I will stay behind this time, but it will be the last time. I need to do something; I feel so useless."

"I understand. I won't leave you behind again, my friend. I have to go and get ready, can you check in on Rose and Benny. They've not been about much; I don't need to worry about them, too."

"Of course, Xander. Be safe."

"Always."

KAS

I watch the brothers leave before turning to Jackson. "What exactly was that?" I ask.

"I don't understand why we're running second fiddle to their kind. We stay out of their problems, and they leave us alone. That is how it meant to be. Why should we help them? I'm not the only one who feels this way, Kas. You can't expect us to feel any different. Not after everything."

"I expect you to follow orders," I shout, slamming my hands down on the table. "Last I checked, I was your

164

Alpha, and unless your challenging that, I suggest you accept your place and do what I ask."

"It is not a challenge – not yet, but change is coming, Kasabian. I only hope you're as ready for it as I am."

"Do not wish to presume you know anything, Jackson. Gather the pack. I think it's time for a reminder of what we stand for," I order.

He leaves the room with his head held high in defiance. I slump down into a chair. *Jeez, I'm getting too old for this crap.* I scrub my hand down my face and lean back, trying to relax before I have to go and do battle with my pack. I knew helping Xander and Kaden wouldn't exactly be a breeze with the pack, but I also didn't expect it to be my Beta stirring up trouble. I let out a deep sigh before standing. Making my way outside, I pull my hair back with a leather throng to keep it out of my eyes. I head to the edge of the forest, which surrounds the reservation: the reservation I built to keep my people safe. The forest circles us almost entirely. The rest of the world doesn't bother us in here. I walk on the trodden path to the clearing we use for our meeting place. It opens up before me and I sit on the wooden log laid at the top for the Alpha. I spend many minutes looking out across the meadow. The wildflowers sway with the grass and the leaves of the trees dance in the wind. I close my eyes and just listen; the sounds out here soothe me. My heart rate slows and the traces of anger filter out and down into the earth. Mother nature centres me. I look up to the clear blue sky above me and see a lone eagle searching for prey; nature at its most simple. When did things get so complicated? Did we make it this way? I sit back and enjoy the calm the outdoors grants me. The silence is only interrupted by the rustling of grass and the sound of children playing in the distance. Looking up, I see my nephews burst from the tree line. Kyle is chasing Tyson. I laugh at their innocence as Ty runs towards me, seeking safe ground. I grab him by his small waist and sling him over my shoulder.

"Uncle Kas! That's cheating, I can't catch him up there," Kyle groans at my feet, his arms reaching up for his brother as he tries to jump up to my height. At age six, he is starting to become his own person, he is definitely an Alpha in the making.

"Now then, Kyle, what have I told you about being a big brother? You are meant to help your little brother. Not chase him!" I say with a stern voice, which my smile makes ineffective.

"But I was helping him! I was teaching him to run fast like me!" he says proudly. I can't help but chuckle at the cheeky grin on his face.

"Boys! I thought I told you not to bother your Uncle," Dani says coming into the clearing. Kyle hides behind my legs while Ty tucks himself into my chest.

"They're okay, Dani, they aren't bothering me at all. Much the opposite," I say, bringing Kyle back to my front and ruffling his hair with my hand. "You here for the meeting?"

"Yeah, I figured you'd want some solidarity. A reminder that you're not alone in all of this."

I put the boys down and bring her close, kissing her hair. "Thank you, Dani. How has everything been with our guests?" I enquire.

"They seems nice. I've not spent time with everyone yet."

"No? I did notice you spending quite a bit of time with one of them though," I say rising my eyebrow at her in question.

A blush creeps up her neck and spills across her cheeks. Since her husband was killed, she's been lost. She's been a great mother to her boys, and has kept things going when I've been needed elsewhere, but she never seems to do anything for herself. It's nice to see her re-joining the world of the living.

"I...he... just, Dimitri – he's easy to talk to. I can't really explain it, but I guess he makes me... feel," she whispers, looking up at me with wide eyes.

"Aaron would have wanted you to be happy, Dani. He was my best friend, and losing him hurt us all, but he wouldn't have wanted you to die alongside him."

She nods as a lone tear runs down her cheek. She wipes it away quickly before gathering up the boys and sitting down beside me on the tree trunk. The pack begins to filter into the meadow, everyone taking a seat depending on their place in our hierarchy. It's an archaic way of life, but it's one that works for us here... Jackson is the last to join us, and that fact isn't missed by a soul here. It's a minor display of insubordination. *Just what I need right now.*

I stand and the murmuring across the group stops, the only sounds are those from the birds and the trees that surround us.

"I know many of you have questions as to why I have made the decision to help our guests, but have not felt able to come and ask me directly." I pause, looking them in the eye. "As I told you all some nights ago, our help is needed to recover a young girl who has been taken. I understand some of you feel it is not our place to intervene – that it is the business of the Fallen; that we should keep to ourselves."

"Too right!"

I hear someone yell out. I turn in the direction of the voice and shout, "Well you are wrong!" my voice booms across the opening. "What I could not tell you the other night, because it was not my place to, is that that girl has an affinity to my wolf."

168

The gasps from the crowd stop me. I had known it wasn't going to be an easy speech, but I had underestimated their response. I clear my throat and continue, giving them no more time to get themselves in a frenzy. "The girl in question is the Chosen One. She is part Fae, part Fallen, and I have spoken to her with my mind. She is the Reborn. This is why we include ourselves in the business of the Fallen, because it is not just their problem. If Cole is able to unleash her power, and use it for his own good, he will wreak havoc across the earth, scorching everything in his path. That includes us and everything we hold dear."

Whispers start back up among the pack, and I hear questions fired rapidly to each other.

I need to be strong. "This is not a time to panic, brothers and sisters. This is a time to call upon what our ancestors taught us. What they passed down to us. It is time to fulfil the destiny fate has set out for us. If we stand united, we shall stand strong."

Jackson stands up and says, "I still don't see why we should fight for them. Why should we sacrifice? Why should we play second fiddle to them? They're filthy creatures, not even from this earth. Why should I take orders from them?"

"You take orders from me!" I shout. Silence descends across the meadow. "Unless you wish to take that power from me, Jackson, I suggest you fall in line."

"And if I don't want to?" he says jutting his chin out in defiance.

"If you do not want to, then we shall settle this the old way," I roar, standing tall and transforming my hands and teeth to those of the wolf. I feel him stir inside me, ready for a fight. Jackson steps backwards and my wolf growls through me until he submits.

"Does anybody else have a problem with my decision?" I look across my pack, making my will known. No-one says a thing; most have their eyes to the floor. I turn to Dani who grabs the boys' hands and follows me out of the clearing. I calm myself enough to appear myself again by the time we come back to the reservation.

"Well, that could have gone better," Dani remarks, sarcasm dripping from her words.

"No one died, so it could have been worse," I say, smiling.

I head back and look for Dimitri. I know how close he and Dani have become in the somewhat short time they've been here, but who says love is measured in time, maybe a week is enough time. I've never been so lucky to experience love so I can't know – and I can't judge. I just want to make sure he'll watch out for her while I'm gone. She's still so fragile after losing her mate. I know she acts like it doesn't bother her, but I know she's still healing. I also want to know how serious he is about her – she's my little sister, and after everything, the last thing she needs is some Fallen bastard messing her about. Don't get me wrong, Dimitri seems like a solid guy, but I don't know him and that makes me wary.

I round the corner of the main building and find him sat comforting Rose. I stay back and watch them. He seems genuine in his concern for her and Addie. He's appeared aloof since his arrival, but I'm beginning to think the step back he's taken has more to do with being here than who he is. He seems to understand that all of this is bigger than his wants and needs, and I respect him for that. He lifts his head and sees me watching him, raising his eyebrows in question. I walk towards him and smile down at Rose who is crying.

"Are you okay, Rose?" I ask.

She clears her face of the rolling tears with the back of her hand. "Yes, sorry. I didn't mean…"

"There's nothing to be sorry for, dear girl. Cry if you need to and don't mind me. Would you mind if I stole Dimitri for a few moments though?"

"Oh, erm, no of course not. If it's okay with him I mean. I can go back to my room." She looks to Dimitri for his guidance.

"It's fine, honey. You go back. You know where I am if you need me, okay?" Dimitri says this to her with the same warmth in his eyes a father would have when looking at his child. He hugs her before she goes and then stands to greet me.

"Kas, what can I do for you?" he asks

"I was coming to speak to you about Dani."

"Oh God, not the big brother talk?" He laughs and I join him.

"Not quite, but maybe a little – yeah, I won't threaten to break your legs or anything though," I chuckle.

"Oh good. Seriously though, man, what's up?" he asks.

We start to walk along the tree line at the edge of the reservation out of hearing. This is more awkward than I had anticipated. "I know you and Dani are getting… closer, and I just wanted to make sure you'll look out for her when I'm not here – while all this shit is going down."

He turns to me, his eyes wide with honesty, "Sure, man – of course! It's not something you even need to ask."

I smile. I'm beginning to really like this guy but he still needs to know that when it comes to my sister, I've got her back. "I also need to make sure you know she's not healed yet," I say. "Not after Aaron died. He was a good man, and a great dad to their boys – but I don't think he was such a great husband to her. He put the pack first, which made

172

him a great enforcer, but not such a great mate – plus his mother was a raging bitch."

"I know all about Aaron – and his mum. I'd like to give that woman a piece of my damn mind. Dani sat and explained everything to me a few nights ago after Ty mentioned him. She was almost apologetic, which I didn't understand at all, but then she explained a few things about their relationship. Trust me, I know she's still broken – and I'm all too aware of how fragile she is. I'm not looking to do anything but help her heal."

"I can respect that, but I had to say. She's my sister ya know?"

"Oh, I know that feeling, man. I've been around Addie since she was ten. I've watched her grow up, and she's like my little sister, too. That's why I'm here. Dani was a nice surprise, I won't lie. Addie will love her – and the boys."

"We'll get her back, Dimitri. Everything is going to be fine. You'll see."

"Have you been able to speak to her again?" he asks.

"I have not, and not for lack of trying either," I answer honestly.

"You know Rose and Xander managed to get to her? But something went wrong, and no-one has any idea what."

"Yes, I heard. The girl was foolish, she could have gotten them all killed, but I understand why she took such risks. I will continue to try and reach her with my wolf."

"Thank you, Kas."

AEVEEN

There is so much to learn in this world, I almost miss my oblivion. Emotions. Politics. Choices. Trying to work out who I can actually trust around here other than Cole, is tough. He's already warned me people would try to get on my good side because of who I am to him. Apparently, being his daughter earns me a high standing. I'd rather be able to fade into the background and observe people, but this is what I've got and I'm not going to waste it. I've spent too long locked away to waste this chance. I have at an actual life. I never knew if I'd ever get this chance so I don't intend to quash it.

Cole introduced me to a few people, Olivia obviously, then his Lieutenants. Each of them were polite. I remember them from before, when I was with Addie. Then he introduced me to Eli, and I'm not sure what to think of her. Cole told me she is delicate, that the Fae broke her long ago, which explains the crazy look in her eyes. She seems almost childlike and Cole cooed over her as if she were a doll. She looked at him like he was her whole world. I'm not sure what happened, he didn't elaborate, but he said she was key to his plans – so I need to get along with her.

Now, I'm sat in a field watching hundreds of Demons and Shades train. I was training this morning, but I was vindicated - it was clear within moments that I don't need training with my powers; Addie was the one who couldn't control them. I am my powers; they are part of me. Using them is the same as walking and breathing for me. It's the combat skills I struggle with the most, which is why I'm sat here watching what Cole called, 'the cannon fodder' train in hand to hand combat. I'm meant to be studying their movements and techniques but I get distracted by the world surrounding me.

This field is huge; I don't know the words to describe how big it is. An open space, protected by huge trees and bushes that continue for miles around our boarders. It's almost as if someone cut a hole in a forest and plonked us here. Mind you, knowing Cole, that could be exactly what happened.

A bell sounds and everyone stops fighting and starts to make their way back into what Cole calls the house, but to me it seems more like a hotel. A building with this many rooms, and this many people, is not a house. I wait up on

176

my hill until everyone is gone. The noise of fighting has finished and now it's peaceful out here. I lie back and stare up at the sky, watching the clouds roll by.

"You okay out here?" I look up and see Logan stood over me. His face is taut, as if he's fighting an internal battle over speaking to me.

"Fine, thank you," I say, giving him the opportunity to leave if he wishes. He surprises me by sitting down beside me, so I sit up and stay quiet, giving him time to speak.

"It's so surreal," he says wistfully, looking out across the field. "Seeing you walking around, hearing your voice, and knowing that you're not her. It just... My mind can't seem to wrap around it. I knew Addie almost my entire life, and now she's gone – but I can't deal with that because you're still here; walking around like it's your right, when you stole it all from her."

He takes a deep breath before pulling up some of the grass and snapping it with his fingers, staring at it intently. "I don't know how Liv does it. She knew Addie longer, loved her harder, but she acts like you're her new bestie – as if you aren't the reason our friend is gone." He stands, agitated. I watch him from the corner of my eye – his level of emotion is curious.

He starts to back away, but there's things he feels compelled to say. "I know everyone expects me to fall in line, and for us to just be friends, but I don't think I can do it."

177

"I don't blame you." I say to him, which stops him in his tracks. "She was your friend – but did you ever know I was inside her? That she was part demon? Micah told me all about my mother, and Cole confirmed it. I know you need to blame someone, and that someone is me, Logan. I did nothing wrong. All I wanted was to be free."

"I didn't know, but what gives you the right to take her away? You must be a demon, because they're the only ones I know who would feel so self-righteous about something so heinous," he says vehemently before running off.

I can't say I'm surprised by his outburst, but I do feel a little sad which shocks me. Maybe Addie's emotions are filtering through. I know from Addie how loyal a friend he is and how kind he can be. I had hoped we could be friends.

I get up and make my way inside, everyone I meet on the way to the sanctuary of my room, says hello. I close the door and lean against it, trying to navigate this life is exhausting. I fight to push down all of the emotions that swirl inside of me. I'm almost afraid to let them out. I let small trickles out, enough so that I can function in this world, but if I let them all out I think I might drown.

I've not heard or felt Addie since I broke free. I have no idea if she's still in here. And regardless of what Logan says, I do feel sad about that. I've also known Addie our entire life, too. We grew together. I felt every grazed knee, every crush, every broken heart. Now she's gone, and it's strange to be alone in here. Even if I couldn't talk to her, I took comfort in knowing she was there, hearing her, seeing things through her. Its things like this that make me feel like she might still be here with me. Emotions are so foreign to me, to feel anything so distinctly of my own violation is unlikely. Everything I ever felt, I felt because of Addie, or so I thought. The emotions filter through at the most unexpected of times. The uncertainty of it leaves a bad taste in my mouth. It feels as if I lost a part of myself, but I can't be sad about it otherwise what did I fight for? It's as if I'm a walking contradiction, like I'm still not my own person. Will I ever be free of her?

KADEN

I'm laid face down on the ground alongside Kas and Xander, and we're looking over to the place Cole is hiding out. We are watching the hundreds Cole has gathered, train. Their numbers are enormous. I see the grim look on Xanders face, and I know he'll wonder if I knew about this. If I was part of this – and maybe once upon a time, I was; but that time has passed. Addie changed me.

I can see her from here, perched up on a hill on the other side of us. From the way she's sitting, she doesn't look like she's in pain; she looks as if she's intently watching everyone below her. It makes no sense – surely if she were free like that, she would leave.

"We need to find out more, this is useless. She's right there. Something is wrong," I say.

Xander doesn't take his eyes off her and his voice is robotic. "Maybe we're too late. Maybe he told her he was her father. All this proves is how little we know – we can't do anything; we'll just get people killed."

His sense of failure frustrates me. "Come on, brother. She's right there. We could just go and get her and bring her back with us!"

"You think I don't want that!" he says between clenched teeth. "LOOK AT HER! Something isn't right. The Addie I know wouldn't just be sat watching a fight. She'd be in the thick of it, telling them to pick up their balls and man up after she pins them. Something is wrong, and if we just go in there, who knows what damage we'll do. I want her back just as much as you do, more so even, but I'm not willing to put her in more danger to do so. You're too rash, Kaden, too quick to act. This needs thought, finesse, not brute force."

"And I suppose you're the great thinker here right, big brother? Maybe you just don't like it because I said it first. This isn't about us, it's about her!"

"Maybe we should go back and regroup," Kas says, trying to diffuse the tension. "We need more details and information before we make any decisions."

"I have an idea, although I don't think either of you are particularly going to like it," I say as we stand and head back toward the reservation.

"Well?" Kas asks

"Let me go in undercover – as if I'm going back to Cole," I say. "As if I'm sorry I lost my temper with him. Let me see what I can find out. I'm the only one who can do it without too much suspicion."

The look on Xanders face cuts me deep.

"I don't know, Kaden," he says. "What if he knows? Then he will capture you as well. We can't afford to lose you."

"What if he doesn't go in alone?" Kas suggests. "Michael and Celeste could go with you. Taking them with you as recruits gives you numbers, and it might even show Cole you're being true. You are not exactly known for being humble, Kaden, so to apologize to him, and take back your actions in front of your own people. It might carry more weight."

"You're probably right," I say sighing. "Argh, I bloody hate grovelling, but if that's what she needs, then I'll do it."

Xander still looks sceptical.

"Come on, brother. Do you see any other way for us to get the information we need? I want her out of there as much as you do."

"You have no idea." Xander growls before stalking off ahead of us. His jealousy is becoming a block.

"Good to see you guys are on the same page," Kas chuckles.

I shrug. "He didn't want to come to me for help. He had no choice, he doesn't understand…"

"I'm sure he didn't, and even if you two have cleared the air, this will still be hard for him. What happened between you both, hurt him deeply. I've been speaking with Dimitri. He said Xander never really woke up again until *she* was born; she gave him purpose. I think at first, it was a protectiveness then it grew into something more. I only know what you've told me about your time with her, but I think she affected you in the same way she did him. That's going to be complicated – no matter what. But none of it matters if she doesn't come home. You both know that."

"I won't lie," I say, dropping my voice so Xander can't hear our increasingly dangerous conversation. "Yeah, she did change me – she reminded me of the life before – but that's all," I protest. "I just want to help."

Kas raises his eyebrow as if he doesn't believe a word I say. We walk the rest of the way back in silence. It doesn't take too long, and the walk helps my plan formulate better in my head. Now I just need to get Xander to agree.

Aeveen

I've been making the most of my time here, watching the different people around me; reacquainting myself with the way the world works. I've slowly started to remember everything I was never meant to remember. My life before. It feels strange to remember who I was, and to be who I am now. It has been so long since I walked this earth, when I was here last the Fallen and the Vampyr Shades did not roam this realm; the world was run by humans and we let them be. It is only now, as I run through the memories of the girl whose body is now mine, I realise how far this world has fallen. I'm curious to find it saddens me that she and I are no longer one, but I have not yet remembered how to bind us together. Maybe in time, but for now, she is still quiet. Maybe she has quietened for good.

"Aeveen, are you hungry?" Olivia asks. She is my friend. I think. I will not trust her, as I trust no-one here. These creatures have proven themselves to be ever fickle, but she, at least, seems to have good intentions. I shake my head and stay curled up on the sofa in the main room. Then there is banging on the door. Olivia strides over and opens it.

"Jackson? What are you doing here? He's going to be furious!"

"I had no choice. I need to speak to him, it's important."

I have not heard this name before. He is new to me. The door widens and Jackson comes in, his worried eyes darting across the room, unable to settle on any one thing until he sees me. His dark eyes grow wide.

"Is that…?" he stammers before Olivia slams her hands into his back.

"None of your god damn business! Now move your ass. You wanted to speak to Cole, not our guests," she spits before jamming her hands into his back again, making him trip forward back out of the door.

"Who was that?" I ask Logan, who is perched next to me.

"No-one important. Just another of Cole's many dogs. The guy has people all over the world who whisper to him. I guess that's what happens when you basically run Hell for a few centuries." He shrugs and leans back.

"Is Addie still here?" he asks suddenly.

I can tell he's afraid of the answer. "She's still quiet," I explain, standing. "I don't know what's happening, I can't tell you anymore."

I make my way down the hallway back to the bedroom Cole assigned as mine. It's right across from his new office. As I reach my door, I'm stopped by the sight of Cole's door not being shut properly and the sound of vicious whispered noises. I make sure not to make a noise as I stand in the hall, listening.

"They're up to something. They're working with Kas, and as much as I try to persuade Kas not to get involved, he's an old friend of Xander – he's having none of it."

I hear a faint voice in my head. "Xander?".

"Oh there you are little bird. Is that what it takes to wake you?" I think.

"Where is Xander?" she asks.

"I don't know Addie," I whisper.

I wait for a moment and I'm met with silence again. I have missed the rest of Cole's conversation, but I can hear them moving about, so I slip inside my room before I'm discovered.

KADEN

It's taken two days to get everyone on board and get the details settled, but Michael, Celeste and I are heading to Cole's tonight at sundown. I'm in my room quietly preparing myself, when a quiet knock sounds before the door opens. It's Xander. I wave him in. He looks so torn up right now, I still can't get over how much this is all affecting him. I know how much he hates that he's not the one going in.

"Are you ready for this, Kaden?" Xander asks. "Like really ready? I know it's been a long time since we fought on the same side, since we relied on each other, but I really need you right now," he says.

The vulnerability in his voice floors me. It hits me just how much he loves her. It kills me, because I know deep down that if I let myself admit it, say I love her, too, it would be irrecoverable. I can't betray him like that – not again.

"It has been a long time, but I've got this. I'm not risking too much; I'm just gathering information. Don't get me wrong, if I can get her without getting us all being killed, I'll bring her back with me – but I won't do anything reckless," I say.

He relaxes a little and pulls me into a hug.

"Thank you, Kaden. Thank you." He says before leaving the room.

Michael finds me a few minutes later sat on the bed, my head in my hands.

"You ready to leave, Kaden?" he asks, looking me over like I'm going to break. I take in a deep breath and push everything down.

"Ready as I'm going to be. Let's get this show on the road." I put on my leather jacket and pull my beanie down over my head. I catch myself in the mirror, my white t-shirt stands out against my black leather jacket. My faded blue jeans sit on my hips and finish sat on my black leather boots. I look like myself. No pretentiousness. Michael is topless, but that's his way. He wears his ink proudly, I'm not sure I've seen him wear more than a jacket in a long time. We meet up with Celeste in the meeting room, and she looks as stunning as always. Her long red hair falls in waves down her back. She's all in black.

"Going for the cat-woman-look, love?" Michael jokes.

"Eat me," she retorts with a smile on her face.

"Good to see some things never change," I say before heading down the stairs and out to the square where I find Kas, Jackson, Xander and Dimitri waiting for us. Dani is hanging on to Dimitri's arm. *Huh… never saw that coming*. Kas walks forward and puts out his arm, which I grasp. He clasps my shoulder and draws me in – this feels too much like goodbye.

"Good luck, brother. Come home safe," he says before stepping back.

"I will. We shouldn't be gone more than a few days. If we're gone more than a week, then you can worry. Otherwise, we'll see you soon," I say, unfurling my wings through the hidden slits in my jacket, relishing in the freeing feeling. Michael and Celeste do the same and we push off and soar into the darkness of the night.

COLE

I pace back and forth behind my desk, waiting for the final pieces to fall into place in my mind. Everything is falling into place, but each string of the web is so intricate, each piece balanced – dependent on another string holding strong. Aeveen has awoken, but she is not going to be easily deceived; not like Adelaide. She is the Reborn, and once she remembers exactly who she is, I have a feeling she's not going to be easily swayed. I need her to become attached to me before then, then she'll already be on my side. I need to tread carefully. Play the long game and keep my temper in check.

The door to my office swings open, showing Suki stood in the doorway arms crossed, looking more than a little pissed off. I roll my eyes at her. What the hell did I do now?

"Suki, it's wonderful to see you in such a pleasant mood. Please, come in."

"Don't fuck with me, Cole. Not today," she says strutting into the room and slamming the door behind her.

"And what, pray tell, has you spitting feathers today?"

"I just saw your little protégée and I'm worried. I think she's remembering. She doesn't practice fighting because she feels at one with her powers. Her eyes become older each day as knowledge trickles from her subconscious. We cannot trust her, and we cannot rely on her," she says, pouring herself two fingers of scotch from my decanter. She always was brazen.

"Help yourself. Look," I say, trying to hide my own concerns behind bravado, "you don't need to worry your pretty little head about it. I have it all under control."

"Are you kidding me?" she scoffs. "You're losing control a little each day, Cole, but your so blinded by a desire for vengeance, you can't see it! You're playing with fire using her this way. She could destroy us all."

I rush forward and grab her by the throat, my hand squeezing her delicate skin as I lift her from the floor. Her fingers claw at my hand as I hold her suspended.

"Do not think to tell me what to do, Demon. You forget your place!" I spit before throwing her across the room. "You may be a ruler of Hell, but you *will* bow to me."

"Forgive me, Sir," she says, her head bent in submission. "I did not mean to overstep. I am simply concerned."

"It is not your place to be concerned. Leave me," I say, turning my back to her and gazing out of the window until I hear the door click shut.

I watch as my drink swirls around in the bottom of my glass. The amber liquid burns as it goes down; the taste is strong and smoky-sweet. I savor the taste before swallowing. I'm waiting for Olivia and Micah to grace me with their presence. I've been unsettled by Suki's earlier observations, and I want reassurance. This day has been too long already and I'd really rather get this out of the way sooner than later. In fact, I'd rather be anywhere but here, but these two have been, and continue to be, pivotal if everything is going to fall into place. I lift my head, glass in hand as they enter the room. Olivia closes the door behind them. They walk across the room in silence, each looking at the floor before stopping in front of my desk, which I'm sat behind. Apparently, news of my mood has spread across the compound.

"Updates?" I ask. They both begin to speak before quieting when I raise my hand. "Micah, you first."

"Yes, Sir. Aeveen is now awoken as you are aware, so I've taken up my role again in training the Demons and Shades ready for the new war. The Demons, unsurprisingly, don't require much work. The Shades, however, are another story; they're unruly and ill disciplined, which I suppose is their nature. They will be better used as a distraction than a decent fighting force."

"Well done, Micah. Hopefully, we will not need it, but it's good to have a contingency. We won't use the Shades unless dire circumstances come to light. Now, Olivia?"

"Thank you. Aeveen appears to be adjusting well. She has been reasonably quiet, but no more than to be expected. She's been very inquisitive about certain things, emotions more than anything. She seems very conflicted about it all. I think dealing with her Fallen side, with the remains of Addie's emotions, has all been a bit much, but she seems to be coming out the other side of it. Her and Logan are growing closer, although she still keeps us all at arm's length. As I said, she's conflicted. The only thing I am sure of, is her loyalty to you. We tested her by having a couple of Demons talk about dissention; they're now recuperating in the med wing."

"Excellent," I say clapping my hands together. "I plan to use her to get to Xander and Kaden. She will go back to them and infiltrate their ranks, gain their confidence before turning on them. Her role is to slay them in the dead of night, when they are least expecting it. It will be glorious. To know they're finally gone - to the hellish depths they deserve," I say with a growl.

"How do you intend to do that? Her eyes give her away instantly," Olivia asks.

I grind my teeth between my clamped jaw before I bite her head off for daring to question me. Instead, I take a deep breath and let it out slowly. I'm satisfied to see her wincing.

"They will know she is changed, but she will be adjusted enough to act as if she is Adelaide, and that she has merely merged – their love will make them see what they want to see."

"Will they not be suspicious of her return?" she asks timidly.

I slam my hands on my desk and stand. I let the minx get away with her first challenge – but I cannot have her make a habit of it. "You dare question me, girl!" I roar, causing her to shrink back. "Why would they suspect it if they think they rescued her?"

"I just want to have a clear view of everything. I want to make sure Aeveen knows her part to play thoroughly. How will she kill them? I did not think the Fallen could be killed. I thought they were Immortal," she asks. Curiosity really is going to kill this cat.

"Immortals are never truly immortal. Everyone has a weakness; it is just a case of knowing what it is. In this case, I'm at an advantage," I say smirking. I push the buzzer on the intercom.

"Ruby, will you join us, please. Oh, and bring *it* with you – Aeveen, too," I order. The room is silent whilst we wait, and I pour myself another drink. Eventually, a knock sounds at the door and Ruby enters the room with Aeveen in tow.

"Ladies! How nice of you to join us," I say with a genuine smile on my face. Knowing how close I am to finally having my revenge on Xander is liberating. Freeing almost. "Please, sit."

I return to my seat behind my desk and motion for them to sit. Aeveen sits quietly, taking everything in. She observes each person in the room, the only emotion she betrays is the fire that lights in her eyes when they brush over Micah. There is still anger there, even though she is aware that what was done had to be done to set her free.

Interesting. Ruby sits down, poised, as if she's ready to strike. Her long dark hair pools on her chest, accentuated by the black corset she's matched to her skin tight black jeans and thigh high leather boots. She takes herself and role seriously. The silver chain wrapped around her wrist and up her arm, doubles as a whip. Few know just how deadly she can be with it. She places a polished wooden box she brought in with her on her lap, clasping her hands over the top of it protectively – as if her life depends on it, and I suppose that's fitting, because it pretty much does.

"Is that it?" I ask her, wanting her to confirm before my giddiness takes over.

"Yes, Sir. I collected it myself this afternoon," she confirms.

"Did you watch its creation?" I ask with anticipation. The completion of my plan pivots around the piece.

"I did, Sir. It was done in the old way," she confirms.

I can't stop the glee that courses through my veins.

"What is it?" Aeveen asks.

"That, my dear, is the weapon forged especially for you. The only thing that can truly kill a Fallen."

I take the box from Ruby and open it. The pointed blade sits on blood-red velvet. I lift it out carefully, sure not to cut myself on it. "This is a blade made of iron. Iron forged in the blood of the Fae; the only weapon known to kill one of us - except of course, you, my dear. But this, this is a guaranteed kill once it pierces the heart," I explain before placing the blade back in its box. Everything is finally starting to play out the way I wanted it to. Now to start the ploy of getting Aeveen back to Xander.

"Why does it need to be me?" Aeveen asks.

I smile at her kindly. She may be a fundamental tool in my vengeance, but she is still my daughter; I can't stop the paternal feelings that sneak up on me when she seems vulnerable. "Because you're special," I say. "You alone are uniquely placed to do this. They trust the body you own. They trust the one who used to reside in it; they will never suspect you will hurt them. It is not just this, Aeveen, I mean it when I say you're special. You are the Reborn. You will discover more power than any other on this plane. They cannot harm you. Even if they try, they will fail. I trust you. I know you can do this."

Chapter Thirteen

AEVEEN

It's a strange feeling, knowing you're being manipulated. That you're nothing more than a pawn. Emotional ties confuse me. I trust Cole; he bought me back to life. He created this body so I could exist. And yet, he wishes to use this body for his own gains. He needs me, and that in itself is potent – being needed. I find it hard to resent being used when I see how much he needs me. I want to please him. I want him to be proud of me; To have no regret over bringing me to life. While I'm not sure he can destroy me, I'd rather not find out. While I remember some things, I do not remember everything I once knew. The dark patches that fill my mind, stay empty, and I do not know if I will ever gain that knowledge back.

After telling me the truth about who I really am, *what* I really am, he dismissed us all from his office while he sat and talked to Ruby. That's how I find myself sat back in the main room at the front of the house, curled into myself on one of the many chairs scattered across the room. The sound of chatter raises significantly and I look up to see the room full of Demons. None that I know, but they are all worked up about something. Whatever it is, I'm going to sit and watch from back here. I'm not a fan of Demons. Even though Micah and Cole convinced Addie she was part demon, I know better. I know I'm part Fallen, part Fae.

Logan sits down beside me, blocking me from view. "I see you also decided to avoid the crazy," he says, turning to me.

"I'm not really sure what's going on," I reply.

"Well, you won't have to wait long to find out," he says leaning back in his chair.

Olivia appears in the doorway and yells across the room, "Alright, you idiots. Calm your shit!" She walks to the main door and opens it to reveal three Fallen. I recognize them from Addie's memories. They are her... friends? How is that possible after they took her? I wonder if I will ever understand emotion fully.

"Kaden, I'd love to say it's nice to see you again, but well, I try to avoid being pleasant to dickheads," she says with a sarcastic smile on her face. The redhead next to him, Celeste, steps forward growling. Kaden puts an arm out to keep her back.

"Now then ladies, play nice. We're here to see the boss," Kaden says before adding a charming grin. "Unless you want to party first, Liv? Vampyr looks good on you." He winks at her and then laughs at her retort which I miss. The male with bright blue hair, Michael, coughs, using his hand to hide his laughter.

"Ugh, fine," Oliva says, scowling. "Follow me. On your heads be it. You didn't exactly leave here on the best terms last time, or did you forget that little tantrum, Kaden?" She becomes more and more flustered the longer they stand there. She turns and waves them into the room. I study Kaden as he strolls in as if he owns the place. He certainly seems to believe his own self-worth. I wonder why Cole wishes him dead; his cockiness is certainly enough to have got on the wrong side of people. He scans the room and while he seems casual, his eyes are calculating. They settle on me, and I see his shock upon seeing me. He recovers himself quickly. His eyes stick on me, and I can't read what I see there.

Kaden? Kaden! Don't leave me here please.
No don't go! Why are you even here?
Kaden!!

I hear Addie's plea's in my head; I can almost feel her desperation and disappointment when the three walk on by and follow Olivia down the hall. I have the uneasy feeling Cole's plan is about to be thwarted. Addie continues to yell inside my head. She becomes so loud; I can't take it. I place my hands on either side of my head and tuck my head in between my knees, trying to shut it out.

"Aeveen are you okay?" Logan asks.

He seems so far away. The incessant noise in my head pushes and pushes me until I can bear it no longer. My scream fills the room. When I lift my head, it is to see Demons sprawled across the floor. Some are bleeding from their eyes, ears, and noses. Logan appears to have passed out and blood trickles from his nose, too. I just wanted Addie to stop. I can't hear her anymore. As I look around the room, I see all the glass from the windows have shattered and is now scattered across the room.

What did I do?

KADEN

It takes every piece of resolve not to turn and run to Addie when I hear her scream. She doesn't look like Addie anymore. Those eyes… they change her entire face. They're so cold and unfeeling. She's still in there, though, I know it. It felt almost impossible not to pick her up and fly her out of here, but I'm here for a reason and I can't forget it. I reach out and stop Liv with a hand on her arm, my face questioning the scream. I don't know what they've done to her. She might not even know me now, and that hurts more than it should. I push all of it down before facing off with Liv.

"It's none of your business, Kaden. Keep moving," she says turning and continuing our journey towards Cole's office.

I haven't really thought about how bad this could all go if Cole hits first and asks questions later. I mean, no, he can't kill me, but there are worse things than death. I take a deep breath before nodding back to Michael and Celeste, then continue following Liv. They're here in case shit goes wrong, and to help scout out the compound. I'm really hoping things don't go south. I don't want to be a screw up again, and I don't want Addie hurt in the crossfire.

I put a cocky smile on my face and walk into Cole's office. Walking straight to the decanter on his desk, I pour myself a drink before sitting down in front of him. A lot of this game is about showing strength, even if you don't feel particularly strong. Michael and Celeste stand by the back wall near the door.

"Nice to see you again, Kaden," Cole says with a sneer. He doesn't seem surprised to see me.

"Ah, come on, man, don't be like that. Let bygones be bygones. Water under the bridge and all that crap. Holding a grudge doesn't become you, mate," I say, taking a swig of the scotch. One thing never changes, the man appreciates a good drink, even if he is a snake.

"What are you doing here, Kaden? You bought your little lackey's too, so I'm sure whatever it is, it's good."

"Oh come on, now. Don't be like that. What's a little disagreement between friends?"

"Get to the point, Kaden." he says. I can see his patience is wearing thin. *Well, this is going splendidly.*

"Fine. My point is, I was wrong, and I want back on the winning team," I say, sitting forward with my elbows on my knees, trying to look earnest. "I tried to be the good guy, turns out it doesn't suit me. The old saying is true; good guys never win – plus, my brother is driving me insane with his holier than thou bullshit. I guess I'd forgotten what a prick he can be. Point being, I want back in."

Cole is silent while he examines me. He's trying to decide if I'm being genuine. I try and contain my growing impatience. Now is not the time for irrational actions. Cole leans back and crosses his arms, a scowl still painted on his face. After a moment of deep deliberation, he stands and barks out a laugh.

"You never were fit for the good-guy-bullshit. You belong here – in the darkness, with me, my friend. We were reborn in shadows. It's home." He walks around his desk and embraces me. "Welcome home. Now tell me about your brother and his plans for his beloved."

I smile and knock back the rest of my drink. "Ah, well there's plenty to tell you about that, but more importantly, I can tell you what his plans are for you."

"Oh really?" he asks, as he sits back against his desk and folds his arms. "And what if I already know them?"

"Well then, lucky you, but I'd ask you how much you can trust your source," I retort. I hadn't even thought of that. He nods towards Liv who leaves the room, sneering at Celeste as she does. We wait mere seconds before she returns, and throws someone to the floor. My shock is evident and I bark out a laugh.

"Well, shit. If you're dealing with dogs, I know you're desperate. Jackson, you idiot! This guy hates wolves!"

"To Kas," I say raising my glass, "the guy with the absolute worst luck in Beta's."

If Jackson's here, then Cole already knows exactly what's been going on at the reservation. I hadn't planned for this – luckily, I'm good on my feet.

"So," I turn back towards Cole. "You already know the majority of what's going down with my brother. Let me just make sure our good friend, Jackson here, hasn't missed anything out.

Jackson eyes me with confusion, which is a good sign. "We arrived at the reservation a few days ago after discovering you were here. Kas has been assisting us. Kas, Xander and I were here a few days ago scouting out your compound – oh yeah, buddy, you've got security issues - Anyhow, after that we decided to send a scout for further information, and they picked me. Nothing like being a good turncoat, hey?"

I finish before draining my glass, then throwing it in the air before slamming it down on the desk. Cole laughs and I feel some of the tension in the room dissipate.

"Kaden, man, you really are something! Jackson, get up off the god damn floor," Cole commands before walking towards Jackson and clasping his shoulder. "At least we know you didn't lie to me." Then, before I even have chance to stop it, I hear the sickening crunch of breaking bones and Jackson falls to the floor, his neck at a sickening angle.

"Who needs traitors in their mix. Filthy animals! He was useful for a while at least." Cole says, dusting himself off before sitting down and pouring us both another drink.

"Olivia, show Michael and Celeste to the guest rooms – and play nice," Cole orders.

Michael and Celeste look at me and I nod, confirming the move.

"And make sure they're fed," Cole adds. "There's nothing worse than hungry Fallen. You'd know wouldn't you." He leers at her with a wink. I see her flinch, but she masks it with a smile and does as she's bid. I wonder what the story is there.

"Welcome back my friend," Cole says raising his glass. "Let the games begin."

Chapter Fourteen

DIMITRI

"They've been gone too long!" Xander says with exasperation. "We shouldn't wait any longer, we need to go in! For all we know, they're all bloody locked up now."

He paces back and forth in front of me and I guard the door to stop him doing something stupid like flying out of here.

"Xander, you need to cool your shit. You're no good to anyone when you get like this. Even if that is the case, we said we'd give them a week. It's been three days; they still have another four days before we need to panic. Kas is already losing it about the fact Jackson is MIA. One of you has to act like a god damn leader before everything falls apart. Now pick up your skirt, grab your balls and man the hell up," I yell at him.

I'm sick of this. I want my friend back, the calm and logical one who always kept himself in check and put the mission first. I know this is different because its Addie, but jeez, I'm tired of it. Don't get me wrong, if it were Dani, I probably wouldn't exactly be Iceman, but I wouldn't be flipping the hell out like Maverick either. Man, you know things are going bad when I start quoting Top Gun. I'm looking forward to things settling down, maybe I'll get Dani and her boys to watch it with me. I realise I've gone off on a tangent and refocus on Xander.

He looks at me and the wildness in his eyes settles a little. I think I might finally have been able to reach him. We've fought together, bled together, and leaned on each other for longer than I care to think about, but this is the first time I've seen him like this.

I know he lost it a little after his sister died, but from what I heard, he threw himself into his work and became the best house leader and warrior most of us have ever known. That's who he was when I met him, so seeing him like this is so out of character. I've never thought it before, but right now I wish Kaden were here. He might be a prick ninety percent of the time, but him and Xander are like two pieces of the same person. If I didn't know different, I'd think *they* were the twins.

"You're right," he says. "I'm sorry. I just don't know how to deal with everything I'm feeling. There's just so much."

"I get it, I do. But find an outlet. Go spar with Kas. Hell, you could both use it, but please – do something other than this."

"Thank you, as always, Dimitri, for knowing how to reach me," he says, before walking around me and out of the door.

I rest my arms on the chair in front of me and let my head hang, taking several deep breaths and trying to centre myself. There's a rap at the door and it opens. It's Dani. She comes behind me, wrapping her warm arms around my waist, kissing me on my back.

"Hey there, handsome. Want some company?" she asks. Her voice is petal soft. It washes over me and soothes my rough edges.

"If it's you, sweetheart, then always," I reply with a light in my voice that hasn't been there before. I turn in her arms and bring her close to my chest, enveloping her. There's something about her that centres me. She smells like spring, like fresh air, and honey and… just Dani. I kiss the top of my head and squeeze her. If I could stay like this forever, I'd take that option in a heartbeat.

"Are you really okay, Tri? It sounded more than a little tense in here." She looks up at me and I lose myself in her deep green eyes for a moment, their depths seem endless.

"I am now you're here. Let's do something," I say.

"Yeah? Like what?" Her eyes brighten at the suggestion. Things have been so heavy here the since Kaden left and we've not been able to spend much time together – and while I've only known her a few weeks, it feels like eternity. She's the missing part of my heart.

"What about taking the boys on a picnic by the falls?"

"Do you think we could? With everything going on, I mean. I feel selfish being so happy when there's so much sadness right now."

I pull her back towards me and place a finger under her chin, tilting it up toward me.

"Never feel bad about being happy, Dani. Few things in this world will bring you joy, savor the good things. Big or small. They're all important. Now come on, let's get those rugrats and head to the falls."

KADEN

"So you tortured her?" I laugh.

"It was needed. You met Adelaide, she was so bloody stubborn, she never would have sided with me against her precious Xander. So I was… let's say I was inventive in ways to get the desired results."

"Well, it seems to have worked. I have to commend you my friend. If I hadn't seen it for myself I never would have believed you'd broken her. Addie seemed so head strong."

"It's amazing what pain will do to a person," he says with a smug smile on his face. I can see Michael behind him struggling to keep his anger in check. These past few days have been a giant test of will for us all. Playing along with his sick game, watching the Demons under his command fight each other for his attention, seeing him play with Addie - because she is still Addie, I refuse to believe any different. Seeing her in action was breath-taking. Watching as she disposed of a group of five Demons that came at her at once, without even breaking a sweat. She really is the Reborn, and she's far more than any of us expected. She's not spoken to me unless I've directly asked her a question. I don't know how deep down Addie is buried, but I have no doubt she's fighting to claw her way to the surface. She wouldn't go down without a war.

"Oh, don't I know it? Torture can be so sweet," I say, almost sick on my own words.

"It can, though I didn't claim the pleasure myself. I let Micah play with her."

"You let that sick fuck at her? Man, that's just evil," I say.

He laughs at me, thinking I'm sharing in the joke, but all I'm really doing is thinking how I'm going to tear the bastard, Micah, apart.

"The means were worth the gains," Cole says. "She might be my daughter biologically, but right now she's just a tool."

I clench my fists under the table out of sight. The thought of pummelling his face right now is so satisfying but I quench the temptation and ask as casually as I can, "What is your master plan anyway? You know I'm here to help however I can. That being said, I do have some business I need to tidy up before I can do much of anything. Playing the good guy left the club in tatters. I need to go back and sort that, apparently there was a death at the mansion I need to clean up."

"Go take care of your business, brother. Come back when you can and we'll get down to the nitty gritty of it all."

I nod and stand. The relief floods through me, and I'm sure it's all over my face, but I can't hide much more. I gather my jacket and head back to my guest room to pick up the stray bits I've got lying around, and instruct Michael and Celeste to do the same. As I'm walking down the hall, I notice Logan hovering by my door.

"I'll meet you guys in ten minutes," I say to Michael and Celeste.

They nod and head off down the hall.

"Logan, what can I do for you?" I ask, surprised he's here. He's avoided me for my entire stay. He's pissed at me and I don't blame him for that. Were our roles reversed, I'd be pissed, too.

"We need to talk – in private," he says quietly. I open my door and wave him in. Following him, I shut and lock the door, before putting on some music on the CD player. You never know who's listening.

"What's up?" I ask.

"I need to know the truth. If you're really here for Cole, or if you're here for Addie?" He asks.

I don't miss the note of desperation in his voice as he says Addie's name. "And if I'm here for Cole?" I ask.

"Then I leave this room right now, and go somewhere very far away."

"You think you can escape Cole?"

"You did once. And anything is better than watching him destroy the people I love," he says with conviction.

"Well, I don't think you need to go to such drastic measures just yet. What do you want from me?"

"I need you to get Addie out of here. Liv too, if possible, but I think she might already be too far gone. But Addie is still there, I see it in Aeveen's eyes sometimes. They gloss over when she can hear Addie in her head. Addie did the same... before. I tried to help her then, but it wasn't enough. She's still in there, Kaden. I just know it."

"Okay, kid, I believe you. Hell, I'm hoping and praying you're right. Just keep your shit together for a little bit longer, okay?" I say.

He looks so desperate that I'm actually worried about what he's going to do. He nods at me before turning and leaving the room. Well shit, I did not expect that. These past few days have totally messed with my mind. *I need to get out of here.* I leave. My guys are waiting just outside the front door. I catch a glimpse of Addie. Logan was right, she does look glassy-eyed sometimes, like now. I shake my head start to run, pushing off and releasing my wings to fly back to the reservation.

I had hoped the journey back would help release some of the tension and anger, which has built up the past few days, but if anything, it's unleashed it all. It's brimming over the edge and I feel overwhelmed by it. I dive when I see the Reservation and come to a landing right in front of one of the wolves, Dani, the one Dimitri's been sniffing around.

"You bloody idiot!" I spit. "Did you not see me coming, you silly bitch – I could have killed you. Or is that what you want?" I tower over her, my anger finally getting the best of me. "I could help you out with that if you want. Poor little widow-wolfy. Want to go see your hubby? I'd be surprised if he wanted to see you since you fucking put him in his grave."

She starts to cry, but I can't seem to stop myself. "Aw, the little whore can't handle the truth, is that it? I'll be surprised if those two boys of yours are even his."

"Kaden that's enough!" I hear Celeste yell as she lands just a few feet to my left.

"Stop being such an ass and apologize to that poor girl! It's not her fault you're so pissed off." Michael berates me. I look at them both and just walk away before I start on them, too. I need to find my brother.

CRASH

Chapter Fifteen

AEVEEN

"I'm surprised you trusted him so easily," I say to Cole, watching the figures disappear in the distance. We're out on the field where Kaden and his friends just left.

"I don't blame you for being sceptical, daughter, but you don't know him the way I do. Kaden's a loyal beast at heart. We've been through too much for him to ever really turn his back on me," he replies.

"Is that why you did not tell him of your plans to kill his brother?"

"Kaden is a dear friend. Killing Xander will pain him, but he will understand. I merely do not wish to cause him any more pain than necessary. Now then, we have much to do. Things have changed, which means so have our plans. Kaden is obviously more useful to me alive, so we have logistics to work out."

"Why exactly is it that you want Xander dead so much?" I ask.

"Xander took something very precious away from me a long time ago. He deserves to pay for that."

"But didn't taking away the woman he loved equal that betrayal?"

"No, it did not!" he roars, before composing himself. "Sorry, but no, it did not. What he took from me, what he stole, I valued more than my own life."

I nod as if understanding, but really, I do not understand his unstable quest for revenge. He is my father so I will help him as any daughter would, but I don't think I will ever understand it truly.

"Please don't let him kill Xander. I'll do anything. I'll never speak again, but please I'm begging you, do not kill him, Aeveen. He is everything," Addie says inside my head.

"Addie, there is nothing I can do. I will not defy our Father. He is the reason I get to live."

"Please, Aeveen. I don't know what I'll do if he dies. I can survive not existing as long as I know that he does."

"Enough, Addie. There is nothing you can do. You had the option to merge with me, for us to live as one and you rejected me. You made your choice. You could have stopped all of this, but you didn't fight hard enough. Now it is time to live with your choices."

"Aeveen. Are you okay?" I shake my head to rid me of her.

"Sorry, Father, yes I'm fine. It's just been a long few days. I should rest."

"Of course. You do that. I'll get to work with the preparations. Kaden won't be gone long."

"Do you really trust someone so fickle, so easily?" I ask. "It seems foolhardy to just welcome him back with open arms after he turned on you once already."

He seems to take this in and mull it over.

"I have no reservations about him, but if it will help your unease, I can send a scout to follow him and report back to us. Will that settle your distrust?" He smiles down at me, as if pleased with himself for discovering a way to placate me.

"Yes, Father, I think that's a very good idea. I don't trust him, or his friends," I reply, smiling a small smile.

"Very well, I'll send someone out at once."

"How could you, Aeveen, Kaden is our friend! You're going to get them all killed!" Addie pipes up again.

"If he is lying to us, then it is his own fault. He is responsible for his own actions. If he's here under false pretences, he isn't here for anyone but you." I push her back down until she's nothing more than a whisper in the back of my mind. I can't wait for Father's plan to be executed so we can focus of getting rid of her once and for all.

KADEN

Kas and Xander pull me upstairs as soon as they discover I'm back, but I can't bring myself to say the words I know will break my brother the way they broke me – *she's gone*. They start grilling me about the layout of the compound, so I bring Michael and Celeste up to help fill in the blanks, Dimitri follows them up, so the whole team is pretty much here.

"So, it's basically a fortress once you're inside the building?" Kas asks.

"Yeah, pretty much," Celeste confirms. "The only advantage we have is that they have almost no security outside – but that means we need to draw them out somehow."

"We can do that easily enough. Cole has never changed. We challenge him," I say. "That will draw him out faster than anything. We've already lost our element of surprise by going in there, and even if we hadn't, Jackson would have given us away anyway."

"Jackson?" Kas asks looking confused, and I realise none of us have mentioned him yet.

"What about Jackson?" Kas asks again looking between us.

"Let me start off by saying, we had no idea when we went in. But Jackson was working with Cole; he's been feeding him information ever since we arrived."

"That god damn asshole!" Kas shouts. "That lying son of a bitch. Where is he now?"

"Dead." Michael answers from the edge of the room. "Cole heard Kaden out, then decided he didn't need two traitors in his midst, so he snapped Jackson's neck. I'm sorry Kas."

"I have the worst luck with god damn Betas! I can't believe he betrayed us all like that. Fucking snake," he says before continuing to cuss him out.

"I'm sorry about Jackson, Kas, but we need to focus. Cole will be expecting me back in a few days and we need to act before then."

"Kaden's right: we need to focus. I'm sorry about Jackson, too. He seemed like a decent guy before this, but we don't have long," Xander says, placing a comforting hand on Kas' shoulder.

"It's not just Cole we need to worry about," I say causing everyone to turn to me.

"If this all goes to plan, and everything works out well, brother, you need to be prepared for the reality that we might not get back the Addie we knew."

"What do you mean?" Xander asks. I feel Dimitri's eyes on me, too.

I look to Michael and Celeste, but they drop their eyes to the floor. No-one wants to be the one to say it.

I clear my throat and consider my words carefully. "When we were there, we saw Addie, but... she wasn't Addie anymore."

"That doesn't make any sense, Xander says, furrowing his brow. "How can she not be Addie? I know she's been through a lot, but she's going to survive this. I know it."

"You're not understanding me, brother. They don't even call her Addie now. I managed to speak to Logan before we left, and as weird as that was, he's as worried as I am."

"Spit it out, Kaden, I don't have time for your riddles," Xander shouts.

"They call her Aeveen now. Apparently, Aeveen lived inside of Addie, she was Addie's power, bound by Queen Eolande, and over the years she became conscious; her own entity, as it were."

"That can't be possible." The shock on Xanders face is concerning. This is exactly why I didn't want to tell him. He's already been emotionally unstable, and I'm worried this might tip him over the edge.

"I'm sorry, Xander. I wish it weren't true. Cole said they were meant to merge, but Addie wasn't having any of it. Stubborn as she is, I can believe it. I won't burden you with the gritty details, but Cole found a way to unleash

Aeveen, and she's currently the one in charge. Addie isn't there."

"But there's a chance they could still merge? Or that Addie could come back?" Dimitri asks as Xander stands, absorbing all of the information.

"I don't know. Cole seemed confident Addie was gone. But he doesn't know her like we do. I think she's still in there, so it might be possible. I can't say for sure."

"Then I will still have hope. This changes nothing. We need to put an end to Cole and his crazy tyranny once and for all. We let things slip recently because he seemed to be keeping the Demons in check for the most part, but this shows me that we've been too lenient with him. This should never have happened. We're going to make this right."

"We're going to need more people, brother. Their numbers are high, and while I'm more than confident in our abilities, and that of the wolves, their sheer numbers are insane. It's as if he's been building an army of Shades, and we all know how many Demons he has at his disposal. The Seven heads of the demon faction all still seem very much on his team, so we have them to contend with too. It's not going to be easy," I advise.

"Nothing worth having in life is ever easy Kaden. Sacrifices will be made, and lives will be lost. Theirs and ours, I'm sure. I will get a message to Marcus; he will help us in this. You know how much he despises Cole."

"I do, although he's not exactly a fan of mine either."

"He will put aside his feelings towards you on this occasion. I'm sure of that. Is there anyone else that you can think of?" Xander asks.

"We could always call upon the Shadows?" Kas says hesitantly.

"I'd really rather not, but we need numbers. Will Jeremy come if you ask?" Xander asks.

"Jeremy is dead. They have a new leader; Shytara. She is a strong wolf and beat him in a call out a few months ago. She's made a lot of changes."

"She? Well, not going to say I'm not surprised by that! Will Shytara listen if you ask her?" Xander asks.

"She's the first female Alpha, and you know the Shadows, they thirst for war. The boys are restless at the peace treaties she's instilled. I'm sure they'll jump at the chance," Kas replies.

"What's to stop them killing us? We're not exactly high on their friends list." It's no secret how much the Fallen and the Shadows have clashed.

"Shytara might not seem like much, but the fact she's Alpha speaks volumes. She's not been Alpha for very long, so I'm not surprised you haven't heard of her. She is fair in her rulings, and brutal in her punishments. The wolves respect her, so you won't have anything to worry about from that perspective."

"Then please call on her. It sounds like we'll need their help. The shadows are nothing if not warriors."

"I couldn't agree more. They have many more experienced fighters than most other packs. I'll send word to her tonight."

XANDER

I head back to my room, no closer to having any form of tangible plan in place. Frustration hits me like a freight train, but I resolve not to take it out on anyone else. I've been doing that too much recently. I need a punch bag to work it out, so I'm heading back to change into a tank and sweats before heading to Kas' gym.

I reach the door when I notice steps behind me. I spin and see Dimitri coming down the hall.

"Are you okay, Xander?" he asks.

"I'm far from okay, but I will be. Once she's back here. I just wish we could come up with a plausible way to get her out of there safely, without having to go to war with Cole."

"I agree, but as it stands, Kaden's idea seems to be the best one we have. It's not ideal, but if Marcus and Shytara get on board, we have the numbers to win."

"And what if Cole didn't buy a word Kaden was saying? What if he's counting on us doing exactly what we're doing?"

"Then we need to deal with it. You could be right; we could be walking into a trap. Addie could die. Any of us could, but unless you see another way to do this, that's what we've got."

"I'm going down to the ring – want to come and spar?" I ask him.

"I can't, man. One, you'll kick my ass and I need to be fighting fit. Two, I said I'd keep Rose updated. Have you seen her when you withhold information? She's definitely a Royal!" he says making me laugh.

"I don't envy you."

"Yeah, thanks. It's going to be a freaking joy. I'm just glad I can escape. It's Benny I feel for. The poor guy can't run away as easy as we can," he says still laughing.

"Poor son of a bitch."

"I'll see you soon, man. Don't kill to many bags, okay?" he says before walking off to see Rose.

Once in my room, I change quickly then make my way down to the gym. When I get there, there are only one or two wolves on the weights, lifting inhuman amounts. These guys look like line-backers: Total powerhouses. They ignore me as I work my way through the main gym and into the boxing gym out the back. Before the dark war, I used to box a lot. I found beauty in the elegance that led to such brutality. How one mis-step, one badly chosen bob or weave, could put you on your ass. Kaden and I trained together for years; it was the one thing we made sure we

222

were always there for. It was our time to just be brothers away from it all. The humans knew no different; it was an ignorant bliss.

I step up to the first bag and start off slow, then pick up my pace. Sweat runs in trails down my spine, but I keep pushing myself. It's times like this, I wish I had my old iPod. Boxing with a playlist was as much an escape as I ever got. After Elaihn, a lot changed, and Kaden wasn't there anymore. Music gave me a much-needed distraction. My mind is one track at the moment, and that track is Addie. I just need to escape my panic for her so I can see the bigger picture and work out how to do this without getting us all killed. I need to be who I was before.

I step back from the bag and grab a bottle of water from the refrigerator in the corner of the room. I pour some over me to help cool me off before taking a few glugs from the bottle. The swish of the door behind me causes me to turn and see it's Kaden, topless and in sweats being followed by Michael in the same get up.

"Oh thank Lordy you're here!" Michael exclaims. "Now I don't need to get my sweet butt bruised. I'm far too pretty to be bashed up. Not that you're not sweetness, too. I'm selfish like that."

I can't help but burst out laughing and it feels so bloody good to laugh.

"Thank you for that – I think," I say. "You wanting to spar, Kaden?"

223

"Yeah, but I know all your moves, big brother, it's almost unfair to you to get your ass handed to you like that. Especially with an audience," he says cockily tipping his head towards Michael.

"It's been a long time since we fought, Kaden; I'm pretty sure I've got you," I reply, confident in my words.

Kaden tilts his head from side to side and bounces on the spot, shaking out his arms.

"You're on, brother. Let's do this."

"Just don't hurt each other too badly. Remember, we still need your pretty faces on the battlefield," Michael says, winking at me before sashaying to the bench at the other end of the room. "I get to play referee!"

We climb into the ring and circle each other for a minute before Kaden strikes, planting his fist firmly in my eye. *Jesus Christ, that hurt!* I zone in on him. We exchange blows, each landing hits and missing some. By the time Michael calls time, I'm bruised and struggling to breathe after a punch to the ribs, while Kaden bleeds from his nose and his eye is swelling.

"So much for playing nice hey, boys," Michael jokes. "It's a good thing you guys heal fast. Kas snuck his head in while you were making each other bleed; he wants to see you both. He has an idea."

"Why didn't you stop us!" Kaden exclaims.

"You needed this, so I let it play out. I bet you both feel better now – so you're welcome. Now go and clean up, both of you, then meet us all in the war room."

DIMITRI

I head to Dani's after the team meeting with Kas, Xander, and well pretty much everyone. The news that came out of it wasn't good, but I think we've got a solid plan now. We're ready. I just need to speak to Dani before I go. If anything were to happen to me and I hadn't said goodbye... and all of the other things that are swirling in my mind, I'd regret it forever.

I may have only known her a few weeks, but I think I knew in those first few minutes that I was lost down the rabbit hole. She stole my heart with that first smile, and I don't want it back. Knowing some of the things she's already been through, I don't want to add to her pain. I just hope she feels the same about me. Jesus, I haven't even considered what I'll do if she turns me down. She's quiet, but behind closed doors away from everyone else, she's spunky – and she has such passion. She keeps me on my toes and usually has me spinning so much I don't know my ass from my elbow.

It's not just her, it's her boys, too. The idea of children had never occurred to me, but those two boys have worked their way into my heart. I don't want to lose any of them.

I round the corner and see her place. My heart is in my throat. I really need to get a hold of myself and calm the hell down. I walk up the path, which leads to her log cabin and knock on the door. Dammit, I feel like a school boy with his very first crush. My palms are clammy and I feel sick. Lord help me, what has she done to me? I hear the family at the back of the cabin; the boys are giving her joyful trouble.

"Dimitri!" the boys yell in sync, leaping on me when they reach me. Thank god for Fallen reactions.

"You boys being good for your mum?" I ask, pulling them each up on my sides. They each groan and roll their eyes at me.

"Yes, Dimitri," they say.

I tickle each of them as they squirm and laugh, trying to escape my grasp. I hear her laugh tinkle over the sound of their snorts. I let them go and they run away.

"Hey, darling" I say, wrapping my arms around her waist. She smiles wide as she puts her arms around my neck and reaches up on tiptoes. I brush my lips across hers. "Did ya miss me?"

"Nope, not even a little," she teases a little breathlessly.

"Oh is that right?" I say, lifting my eyebrow and tightening my hold on her. I spin her around.

"Oh my god! Stop! Put me down you big brute!" she pleads through her laughter. I give in to her wishes and place her feet back on the ground. She's more like a pixie than a wolf. I love how dainty she is.

"What are you doing here anyway? I thought Kas and the guys needed you," she asks.

"They do, but I had to come and see you."

"It's not good news, is it?" she asks quietly, pulling herself away from me.

"Now then sweetheart, don't you be doing that. I'm not going to let a thing happen to you or those boys. It's just I have to leave earlier than we expected," I say sternly.

"How soon?" she asks, turning those big eyes up and me. The emotion swirling in their depths, kill me. I don't want to leave her.

"A few hours. That's why I had to come here and see you. I need you to know I'm coming back. No matter what, I'm coming back for you. You aren't getting rid of me that easily. You got me hooked on you, and I'm not giving that up. I'm not giving you up. You or the boys, do you hear me? You're mine now, and there's no escaping that."

"Dimitri, I…"

"Don't you say it, Dani. I know you're going to try and push me away to protect that heart of yours, but you already have mine. It's yours, and I'll do everything to protect yours, too. I'm not going anywhere."

"Oh, Dimitri, I couldn't stand it if anything happened to you. Please be careful."

"I will be fine, my love. You're stuck with me always."

"I can't lose anyone else I love, Dimitri."

"You love me?" I ask, startled.

"I do, I know people will say it's wrong, or it's too quick, but I do."

"I love you too, Dani," I say. "I don't care what anyone else thinks. As long as I've got you, the rest of them don't matter."

Chapter Sixteen

COLE

"Sir, the scout is back," Ruby informs me. I'm lounging in the main room at the front of the house. Life has been so busy recently that I've had no time to be down here, and now I'm going to have to leave again. I'm so sick of my bloody office.

"Great, I'll meet him outside. I suggest you and Olivia accompany me," I order before heading out to the front court yard. I chose this place out of necessity, no-one really bothers with the wolves, and the wolves and fallen rarely speak these days, so it seemed like the perfect place to escape and build my armies. What I didn't count on was the Fallen and the packs banding together. Whoop-de-fucking-do! Of course they choose *now* to band together like merry freaking men. I hope to god that this scout has good news, otherwise Aeveen was right and I was naïve. It also means with Jackson dead that I've lost my only source of information about what Xander and the pack are up to. Killing Jackson may have been rash, but it seemed like a good idea at the time. I really don't like wolves.

The scout approaches and I can see the worry on his face. Well, shit, this isn't going to be good. Ruby and Olivia flank me, one on each side; the tension is thick.

"Hello, Scott, I assume you have news for me?"

"Hello, Sir – yes I do. I followed Kaden as you asked. The three of them left here and went directly back to the Hunter pack reservation. I stayed and waited to see if he went elsewhere, but after a run in with one of the wolves, he met with Xander and Kasabian. He didn't leave the reservation. There has been a lot of activity at the reservation though. Messengers left not long after Kaden's return, and the wolves that are there seem to be preparing to move."

"Are you fucking kidding me?" I roar, stepping forward and grabbing him by the throat. I see red as I lift him from the floor, squeezing his neck. Pleasure rips through me as I see him struggle to breath, and he tries to fight the grip I have on him. It makes me squeeze tighter as I watch his eyes bulge from the lack of oxygen.

"This is the last time he will betray me!" I shout before snapping the Demons neck with my bare hands. I let him go and he drops to the floor like a sack of lead.

"Was that really necessary?" Ruby reprimands me, and I spin, focusing my anger on her. She raises an eyebrow at me, challenging me, but we both know I need her too much to hurt her. I turn to Olivia who is stood quietly, as if she's trying to fade into the background.

"You! This is your fault! You bought Kaden back to me. Everything was going so well until you bought him up to my office. Since then, everything's gone to shit! I never should have listened to you!"

"But I didn't..." she squeaks before I'm on her. I grasp her by the throat - the last one gave me so much joy, why change a good thing. I watch as she struggles and it fills me with glee, knowing I could end her with the flick of my wrist.

"Cole, will you stop acting like such a god damn baby! Put the girl down, this is not her fault." Ruby yells at me in frustration but it just makes me angrier and I squeeze Olivia's throat harder in defiance.

"For goodness sake, put her down!" she shouts before punching me square in the jaw. I let go of Olivia who falls to the floor gasping for breath. I take a step back, jolted by the power of the hit. Ruby is kneeling by Olivia making sure she's okay when sense descends upon me. I really need to keep my anger in check.

"I'm sorry, Olivia, Ruby is right, this is not your fault, it is mine. I apologize for hurting you."

"It's okay, I'll be fine," Olivia croaks, rubbing her neck as Ruby helps her to her feet. I can already see the purple marks forming on her pale skin making me feel a little remorse.

Suki approaches from the house and sees the mess around me. "Lost your temper again, Cole?" she goads. "Ruby, clean up this mess. You," she points at me, "I found what we've been looking for."

"You have?" I ask shocked. I never thought it was possible. There had been whispers, but I thought they were just that. Excitement flows through me as she nods in confirmation.

"Did you get it?" I ask, impatiently.

"Of course. It's waiting for you upstairs, in the room next to yours," she says with a smug smile. This, this could be the thing to change everything. My secret weapon. My true happiness. I rush inside and run up the stairs. I stride down the hallway and fling open the door of the room next to mine.

The girls standing in there turns and looks at me with a glassy gaze, an innocent smile on her face.

"Coley Bear!!" she squeals, running towards me. I gather her up in my arms and breathe her in. She's really here. This is real.

"You're really here," I whisper, kissing the top of her head. "I can't believe it."

Suki walks into the room and sits on the bed.

"How? How is this possible?" I ask her.

"It seems the Fae don't like to kill; they prefer a fate worse than death. I didn't know her before, but I can tell you she's not the woman you once loved. She has been tortured for hundreds of years, her mind is not really here. She remembers bits and pieces, as you can see, she remembers you. But she's not quite right. She's almost childlike, her mood swings are worse than yours and can happen at the drop of a hat, but she's brutal in the cruellest of ways. I saw her take out one of the Fae when he thought he could take advantage of her while she was half out of it. You need to be careful with her, Cole," she warns me.

"Coley Bear doesn't have to ever be careful with me; he's my big strong man. Isn't that right!" she coos.

"Of course, sweetheart – I'll never let anything bad happen to you ever again," I reply, still keeping her in my arms. I never want to let her go.

"Don't let them hurt me," she whispers. A tear rolls down her face.

"They'll never have you again, my love. They can't hurt you anymore," I soothe.

"I'm going to take that as my cue to leave," Suki says. She leaves me with my gift.

"You're just as beautiful as I remembered, sweet girl," I say, taking her face in my hands and stroking her cheek. She giggles and I can see what Suki means. Something is missing in her. She's not all here.

"Will I always be your sweet girl, Coley bear?"

"Always, Elaihn. Always!"

AEVEEN

I'm resting on my bed, trying to relax after Father created a call to arms. Everything is going crazy outside the door, and I don't really want anything to do with it. I know the part I have to play in all of this, but it seems a bit much. Nonetheless, I will do what is expected of me when the time comes. I just wish we were past all of this already. I want to get to living my life. It feels as if each part of my life is being dictated, and I'm getting close to having had enough.

Someone knocks on my door and I let out a sigh. I really don't want to do anything right now but I get up off of the bed and open my door. I didn't expect to see Logan on the other side of it.

"Oh, it's you," I say.

"Well thanks, it's good to see you, too," he says sarcastically.

"I didn't mean it like that. Why are you here?" I ask.

"I wanted to speak to you. Can I come in?"

"Erm, sure I guess so," I say before going and sitting back on my bed, cross-legged. He comes in and closes the door, locking it behind him, which seems a little weird but he's harmless so I let it go. I watch as he walks over to me, he seems so hesitant in his every move. I wait while he eyes up the bed, deciding whether or not he should sit on it with me, so I tap the bed in front of me in invitation.

"I don't bite you know," I say and he laughs nervously, rubbing the back of his neck. I wait for him to get settled before I ask him again.

"So, what do you want? Sorry, I didn't mean to sound so rude."

"It's fine. I get it. You're still adjusting to everything. And I guess I'm here in one last ditch effort to hope to make you see sense about all of this."

"All of what?" I ask, confused.

"Cole's madness. This stupid petty war, where no-one seems to know what they're fighting for, other than following orders. We learnt history so we would not repeat the mistakes of the past, but that is exactly what is happening here. Can't you see that?" he pleads. "Please reconsider going with him Aeveen. I know you're not Addie, but she was like a sister to me, and I can't help but still think and feel that way when I look at you. I don't want you to get hurt."

I consider what he says. Why are we fighting this war? Cole hasn't truly explained his actions, but then, why should he? He is our leader, my Father. We follow him loyally, as we should. Except, Logan doesn't seem to think or feel that way, and I wonder why.

"Why wouldn't we fight for Cole? He is our Commander," I ask.

"He is not my Commander. I am here through force, not by will. I daresay the same could be true for over half the people down there who are gearing up to fight a war they don't believe in; for a man they don't like. I don't understand it and I won't be a part of it. Please come with me, Aeveen. I could take you to Xander and Kaden. They would keep you safe."

"I won't leave him, Logan. He is my Father. You would be branded a traitor if you left. Are you ready for that?"

"I am considered less than that here, Aeveen. All there is for me here is death. My life is not what I once thought it would be, but thanks to Cole and his warped sense of revenge, I was made a full Vampyr, not a shade. I will not give up what life I have left when he's the reason my life was taken in the first place."

"What do you mean?" I ask. I've not had much chance to speak to Logan since I took over this body, and his story intrigues me.

"I forget you don't know. I was collateral damage in Cole's effort to get you here, Aeveen. Livvy, too. We were killed the first time he tried to capture Addie. I lost my life so he could have you. He didn't care about how many lives were lost in his blindness to reach you. And many, *many* lives were lost in the process. I won't be a part of this madness for any longer than I have to be. I'm leaving as soon as you all start marching. I want you to come with me, Aeveen, please!" he begs.

"I'm sorry for everything you went through, Logan but I won't leave with you. Cole, for all his flaws, is still my father. He gave me a chance at life, I'm not going to betray him now. But I also won't give you away; I know what it is like to be locked into a life you do not wish for. I will not be the one to hold you back," I say to him softly.

He looks devastated at the fact he can't save me, and in turn, save Addie. He gets up and goes to the door, but looks back at me before he leaves.

"I hope everything works out for you, Aeveen. I hope you find peace and happiness. I hope Addie does, too. Mostly, I hope you survive Cole."

LIVVY

Cole has called for war, and that is where we are headed. The Seven are kitted out in full leather battle gear and I'm jealous of it.

"Olivia, come with me please," Cole says from the doorway. I'm in the main hall, alongside everyone else as we suit up ready to march to the reservation. I follow him down the hall to his office where he is stood in front of his desk along with Aeveen, and a blonde woman I've never seen before, but I swear I know her.

"How can I be of service?" I ask wearily.

I don't like going into things blind, and whatever this is has knocked me off kilter. War I was ready for, whatever this is, I don't think I'm going to like.

"Olivia, this is Elaihn; I'm sure she looks familiar to you. Elaihn Bane: Kaden's twin." *Well fuck me sideways. I did NOT see that coming.* There's an evil glint in Cole's eye, softened by a sappy smile when he looks in her direction. *Woah, okay, Cole has a crush. Who would've thought, sure as shit not me.*

"Okaaaaay?" I say.

"While we are out there, she is going to be Suki's ward. With this in mind, I want you by my side at all times. You will be needed to watch my back, and help keep Aeveen safe. You will need to keep us all together."

"I shall do my best, but am I really the best person for this? I mean, I can't even fly."

"Of course you are. If you need to fly, I will personally carry you, but I trust you Olivia, and so it must be you. Do you understand? You will not be going out in the first flank with the Demons to surround the reservation, you will stay back with me."

"I understand."

"This will also keep you safe, Olivia. It is rare that I can trust the people around me. I want to keep you alive," he admits, and I try to keep my surprise hidden.

"Thank you, Cole. I appreciate it. Is that all? I need to finish preparing the others," I say.

"Yes, that is all. Be sure to come and find me once they have left."

"Of course. Aeveen, Elaihn." I give my goodbyes before I turn and leave. I couldn't be more shocked if I became human again. I never even knew Kaden had a twin. How the hell did he keep that quiet? And how does Cole have her now? She didn't exactly seem like she had a full picnic of sandwiches upstairs, but who am I to say anything. Cole seemed positively giddy at having her by his side, and if Kaden and Xander don't know about it, I can't say I blame him.

I'm making my way back down to the front to begin my duties, making sure each demon is fully equipped with gear when a scout comes running down the hall towards me. He stops just before me, his eyes darting from side to side with fear.

"What is it!" I yell.

"They're coming. So many of them. They'll be here within the hour," he says while trying to catch his breath.

"Christ! This day just keeps getting better and better. And you had to tell *me*, so I get to tell him. Delightful. Go gear up," I say to him, standing on a chair and whistling loudly.

"Everybody, listen up!" I yell. "Plans have changed and we don't have long. Get your shit together and get downstairs like yesterday. I'll be back in ten minutes and anyone still here will be flayed and skinned. And not by me! Get to it!"

I jump from the chair and run back to Cole's office, where he's sat in his chair with Elaihn on his lap. Aeveen is perched at the window peering out – I wonder if she can see them? – and the Seven are stood milling around. I guess they like waiting as much as I do.

"Cole," I say cautiously.

"What is it, Olivia?" he asks with irritation.

Why the hell do I have to tell him this. I was almost killed last time. I rub my neck at the thought and my eyes dart to Ruby.

"Erm, a scout just came back and reported that Xander and his forces march this way. They will be here in no more than an hour."

"Xander?" Elaihn giggles. "That's my big brother's name."

"Yes dear, it is," Cole replies softly before looking back at me.

"Is he sure?"

"He looked terrified, Cole. I'm going to say he was pretty damn sure."

"Bollocks!" he yells, which frightens Elaihn, so he takes the time to soothe her before rounding his desk and joining me and the Seven.

"We need to go back to our original defensive plan. We'll go out and meet them, and the rest can wait underground until they are needed," he says, looking to each of the Seven. "Are you ready for this?"

"We would walk through the fires of Hell with you, Sir. We've been ready for this for a long time," Suki replies.

"Then let us go. Tonight, we will bathe in the blood of our enemies and drink in toast to our success."

CRASH

Chapter Seventeen

ROSE

I've never seen the two of them side by side like this. I don't think anyone has in a really long time. They look like the true warriors they are. Complete opposites like night and day. Xanders dark hair with his eyes full of fire, which look as if they will scorch the world to get to her. The leather wrapped around his right arm is an armour I have never seen. A thick brace on his forearm, joining to a piece which looks like dragon scale, melded to his arm perfectly. The black leather straps wrap around his torso from his shoulders to his waist hold his bastard sword, and two smaller daggers. Another two are sheathed in the back of his leather pants. The shadows dance around him as if they are an extension of him. I've never seen Fallen battle, I have a feeling this is going to be something I will never forget.

Kaden stands by the side of him. His blonde hair blowing about in the harsh wind. The sun is hidden by the dark clouds, which have rolled in. It seems only fitting. He is also topless, with two leather braces on each forearm, both armed with a blade. He has two swords strapped to his back. Outwardly, he looks excited; like he's having fun. I've witnessed the darkness raging through him. I know how much he craves the blood lust, the damage he'll inflict. But I know how much he'd sacrifice to make sure she's okay. I've seen the emotion flicker in his eyes when her name is mentioned.

If we all survive this, there is going to be some serious shit to sort through when we're done. I look around at the rest of the warriors; Xanders Elite stand further back with Celeste. Michael and Kas, alert and on edge. Marcus and his Elite even further back than them with Kas' pack hidden in the trees along with the Shadow pack and Shytara. I was pretty surprised when everyone turned up, and tensions have been high at the reservation – but after news Cole would march on us within the day, there wasn't much time for much to be resolved before we started our journey here. I'm hidden, but I refused to not be here– and now we're on the road, heading towards Cole. Attack being stronger than defence. Battle may be no place for a princess, but there was no way I was staying safe in some tower while everyone else went to save my best friend. Benny is hidden with me; I can feel the tension rolling off of

SLOANE MURPHY

him. He's angry I'm here, too, but we both know I'd have been here with or without him.

I hear the gasps before I see her. She doesn't look like Addie. Her beautiful dark hair is now red at the ends, bright like fire, and her eyes glow the same colour, as if her power dances around her. Her face is devoid of all emotion, as if she doesn't even recognize the people across from her. I know she can see them. With her heightened powers, her sight will be as good as the Fallen. I shake my head in disbelief. *What if we're too late? What if she's already gone?*

My breath leaves me when I see Cole stood to the left of her, and then a blonde girl and guy to her right. *That must be Logan and Liv.* Cole leans down to her and says something to her. She nods and steps forward. That's when the ground shakes and I see everyone steady themselves in preparation for whatever hellish thing this is. A huge crevice opens up in the ground and the air fills with screams. Hundreds, if not thousands, of demon horde are running towards Xander and Kaden and everyone else stood behind them.

A smiles dances across the brother's faces and they quickly exchange looks before both running towards the demon horde charging them. I wince as they crash into the first one's they meet. There is such beauty in the way they fight. I don't think they're even aware of how much they work together. They don't look at each other, but they

245

deflect blows and cut through the Demons and Shades in front of them in a way that almost looks like a well-rehearsed dance. Kaden swings a sword in each hand, god-like, he works his way through the Demons and Shades who try to take him down. His wings break free and extend, taking out a few as they come towards him. I watch mesmerized as he flies upwards then tunnel rolls downwards, swords out, taking heads as he ploughs through the horde, which seems never-ending. While Kaden attacks from the air, Xander stays planted firmly on the ground, his sword cutting through any of the demon horde who dare to even look his way.

His muscled torso is painted red and he is completely unfazed by the bodies he leaves scattered on the ground around him. He wears their blood as a medal of honour. Looking back, I see Dimitri, Celeste and Michael all fighting with the same grace as the brothers. The rest of the Elite are clearing up the few who have passed through the first two lines of defence. Marcus and his Elite assess the situation, still untouched by the battle.

Fire screams through the air. One of the Seven women surrounding Cole has broken away, and is launching fire towards our people. I'm up before I think about it, my family descend from a line of water Fae, and if I can help at all, I'm bloody well going to. I launch myself forward, still a distance away but close enough to stop her causing any more damage. Reaching down to the pool of power I feel in my stomach; I latch onto it and lift my arms. Water shoots towards the balls of fire heading in the direction of Kaden and Xander. They extinguish and I can't help but do a little dance before continuing to help out the defence as best I can.

Benny is not happy. "For gods sake, Rose! I can't believe you would put yourself at risk like this! Now they know you're here!"

The adrenaline coursing through me causes me to dismiss his anger. I actually helped them. The demon has retreated, realising she is of no use.

Benny lifts me over his shoulder and runs back to our hiding position. I'm pounding on his back with increasing anger.

The demon horde is almost depleted; bodies lay scattered across the brown wasteland, awash in a sea of red.

There's an electrical hum in the air and the demon elite disappear from view before appearing halfway across the wasteland. I see Xander soar into the air, closely followed by Kaden, before they crash into the ground in front of the Seven; their crash landing creates a fissure in the ground, which separates them. Dimitri and the others land behind them quickly after; Marcus and his Elite follow suit. They've not fought yet but the day isn't over. That's when I see the Shades. Grotesque as ever with their dark grey skin, talons and yellow teeth, they look like the undead they are made to be. Vampyrs not fully made. As almost mindless beasts, they make for the perfect soldiers. They rush forward in a wave towards the group, jumping the fissure in the earth with no mind for their safety, just their mission. The wolves appear in the tree line. I was wondering when Kas would call them forward. The bloodbath unravels in front of me and I hear the cry of a wolf as its overwhelmed by the Shades. I hide my face in Benny's shoulder. I had known we wouldn't come away from this unscathed, but nonetheless, I had hoped.

AEVEEN

I look across the Fallen and feel nothing. They mean nothing to me. All of this is pointless. I don't understand why my Father insists on the killing of those two Fallen. He won't tell me the *real* reason, beyond that they greatly wronged him, and it's their fault we're here.

"Please don't do this," Addie says.

She's been louder today. I can feel her struggling to take over but she isn't fighting very hard so it is easy to keep her subdued. This is my body now. I was repressed for far too long. I will not be pushed back down. She did not wish to merge with me, rejected me and everything we could have achieved together. This is her punishment. I know how much she loves him and I can feel his eyes on me, even though he should be paying attention to the

248

demon whores in front of him. I wonder if he knows he won't be leaving here.

Father searched for a very long time for the iron made with the blood of Fae. It is the only thing which can kill a Fallen. It must pierce his heart to kill him and father is a brilliant marksman. It is only right he kills those that betrayed him. Those that kept us apart. It's all Xanders fault.

"Please stop him, Aeveen. Xander only did what he thought was right. Please!" She screams in the back of my mind. I focus on quieting her again. All that's left is a quiet knocking as she tries to beat down the door between us. Her emotions are pointless.

The fight begins, the Demons going toe to toe with the Fallen and the wolves; it's truly fascinating – almost majestic. Watching them dance around each other, blow for blow. I see one of the Fallen go down, the one with dark hair who has been fighting closely to Xander and feel nothing. These people fight for her, fight for Addie, they don't know me. They just want to use me. But not Father, he told me the truth of it all. He is why I am here now.

I look at the Fallen warriors, and I see Xander take flight. I unfurl my wings ready to head towards him, just like Father asked. He's so focused on me that he doesn't see Father with his bow and arrow. The iron pressed into an arrowhead. I'm aware of him lining up the sight and letting go.

ADDIE

"No!" I scream. The anger pushes me forward. I fight to take my body back. The realization that I could've stopped it hits me as I watch Xander falls towards the earth and I scream out again, claiming my body – pushing hard against Aeveen. I race towards Xander, reaching him just before he hits the ground. I pull him into me, lowering us both to the ground. Kaden roars behind me, but I can't look anywhere but at Xander.

He really came for me, and now he's leaving me.

I lay his body on the ground, keeping his head close to mine as silent tears stream down my face. This is all my fault.

"Xander." I whisper., my tears falling onto his face. His eyes flutter open and my heart soars with hope, before plummeting back down.

"It's really you?" he asks. His question is muffled by the blood spluttering from his mouth.

"It's really me, baby. You just need to hold on and be strong for a little longer, then we can be together again," I say, wiping the steady stream of tears with the back of my hand.

"I'll always love you, Addie – even if I'm not with you. I need you to remember that."

"Don't be silly," I sob. "You're not going anywhere. You're going to be my forever, remember?"

"Addie, I want you to be happy. No matter what." The blood coming from his mouth is now dark and thick. His eyes flutter closed and I'm overcome by sobs, which wrack my body.

This is all my fault.

"Xander, please wake up."

"You wanted us to merge Aeveen, well now's your chance," I say to her. I need her power to reap the vengeance in my heart.

The pool of power in my stomach washes over my body. I turn back to see everyone behind me, with looks of horror on their faces, the sadness and the anger. Rose runs towards us with Benny on her heel. She is crying. Everything is different in the aftermath of merging. It's more. So much more.

Red anger rolls through me. I have only one thought. *Cole*. He did this. He tried to kill me. He used me to get to Xander – and now, he's going to die. I take off and soar into the skies. Cole is in the distance, flying to safety with Liv in his arms. I search through mine and Aeveen's memories to discover his hiding place, but that's soon irrelevant; he's stopped and landed, facing me in challenge. Liv is running. I lower myself to the earth, ready for Cole.

"Well, well, well, it looks like my little girl grew up and finally accepted what she is." He smirks. "Too bad it was too late to save your precious, Xander. That scum deserved what he got. Hell, death is probably too good for him."

I react without thinking and shoot my hands forward; purple fire rips down my arms and straight into Cole's chest. I scream out the anger. The fire intensifies and he's falling back towards to ground – flames ravaging his body. I watch him writhe and scream as the flames eat away at him and I feel nothing. It doesn't take long before his screams die out with the flames. I might not be iron forged with Fae blood, but I am more than enough to destroy one Fallen.

I turn and leave Cole's smoking corpse before heading back to face my grief.

I head back towards Xander and am greeted by a pool of complex emotions.

"We need to get him out of here," Kaden says. "There has to be something we can do." He turns to his people and gives them orders to recover Xander and the other injured from the battlefield.

Everyone jumps at his word. Dimitri takes Rose, and Michael takes Benny, leaving Kaden to carry Xander.

SLOANE MURPHY

I step forward to help Kaden lift Xander from the ground, but he sneers at me. "Do not touch him!" he snaps.

My eyes flash red with the power of the Reborn, giving Kaden no choice but to let his protests fall and step back.

"Shut up Kaden!" I kneel down beside Xander, my arms holding him. "Xander, baby, please – don't leave me. Look at me," I say, lifting his head into my lap. "You can't go yet; it's not time. I love you. I still need you. There's so much we still have to do," I beg as my tears return.

"Addie, you need to let go of him," Kaden says, approaching me with caution. "I need to get him back. I've no idea what's wrong with him – we're not meant to hurt like this. Let me take him. Please?" Kaden asks softly.

I kiss Xanders forehead and wipe some of the dirt and blood from his face before giving him over to Kaden.

Kaden's face is set with determination. "He's going to be okay, Addie. He has to be." He scoops Xander up in his arms and takes flight, leaving me watching them until they are nothing more than a tiny speck in the sky.

"Addie?" Dimitri asks, "Is that really you in there, sweetheart?"

He's cautiously looking me over. I nod.
This is all my fault.

He wraps me up in a hug, and with the comfort of his arms, I shut all my emotions down.

He pushes me to arm's length, trying to find my eyes, but they refuse to lift from the ground.

"Addie, sweetheart, just follow us back and we'll work out what's going on."

He pulls me into another tight hug, before taking flight.

I'm left with the dead of the battlefield and Xanders Elite, who are tending to the injured. I watch as he takes off, and stay behind for a minute looking at all of those who fell today.

This is all my fault.

Reluctantly, I take flight and follow behind, not wanting to face the possibility that Xander might die.

KADEN

"Get the Fae healer here now!" I yell as I land with my big brother cradled in my arms. I refuse to believe he's dying. The wolves gather around me, taking his body from me and rushing him to the medical centre.

"Kaden, what the hell happened?" Kas calls from the edge of the woods. His sister Dani is next to him along with her two boys. They remind me of Xander and I as kids, and I swallow the lump that rises in my throat.

"It's Xander, he was shot with an arrow. Whatever it was, took him down. He's barely breathing Kas... I... I have no idea what to do, help him, please" I say shakily.

Kas walks towards me and hugs me in the way only a friend and brother can. I lean on him for a minute before stepping back.

"I need to go in and find out what's happening."

Kas shakes his head, knowing the sight of what's going on in the medical centre is not something a loved one should witness. "No, Kaden, you wait here and I'll go in and see what's happening. I'll be straight back – I promise."

I watch his back retreat from me into his medical centre. I feel so lost. I thought I finally had a second chance with my brother; to get back to being us. There are very few things that can kill one of us, but Cole would know that. Surely he couldn't find it. We made sure it was gone, but I've never seen Xander take a hit and not get back up. If it's not that, I have no idea what to think.

Celeste, Michael and Dimitri appear in the clearing, followed closely by Addie. I'm conflicted at seeing her. The anger and blame surface. If it wasn't for her, Xander would be okay. He probably still wouldn't be talking to me, but he'd be okay. Then, there's the feelings of love underneath those feelings I dare not explore – or outwardly admit.

My brother loves her. I need to make sure she's okay, too. He'd expect it of me, no matter what.

I approach them with a grim look set upon my face and explain, "Xanders in the medical centre with the doc. There's nothing we can do but wait. He's a stubborn bastard; there's no way he'd let Cole win like this," I say to them, more confidence in my voice than I feel.

I turn towards Addie who looks broken. She's been through so much in so little time that I'm amazed she's still standing. I wrap her in my arms, feeling the tremble of her body as she sobs.

This isn't her fault, really.

"Is he gone Kaden? This is all my fault. I should have fought harder," she says. "I need to get in there. I need to see him. Maybe I can help save him. He can't die, Kaden, I don't know what I'll do if he's dies." She pleads as she pulls against me trying to get into the med centre to be with Xander.

"He's not dying, Addie, just a little broken," I lie trying to convince myself as much as Addie. "We destroyed the only thing that can kill us…"

"Iron forged with the blood of a Fae," she whispers.

Her face is streaked with tears. All at once, her eyes fall on something behind me. The look of despair on her face causes me to turn and I see Kas stood in the doorway of the medical centre. The look on his face slays me.

It can't be.

He can't be gone.

Xander?

THE IMMORTAL CHRONICLES #3
Coming early 2017

There is only so much one person can endure before they break.

There was nothing I ever wanted less than to be Princess at the Royal Court. After devastation rocked my whole world, the return of my mother doesn't seem like the dream it was supposed to be.

I know how to be a warrior. I have no idea how to be a princess...

With her whole world turned upside down, and her heart still broken, who will Addie be at the end of it all?

Hearts can break, faith can plummet, but souls can Soar.

Also by Sloane Murphy

The Immortal Chronicles

Descent

Crash

Soar

Rapture

Of Fire & Frost

A Princess's Duty

A Kings Oath (Coming Soon)

Standalones

When We Fall

CRASH

Thank you so much for taking a chance on Addie &
Xander. I hope you enjoyed reading them as much as I
enjoyed writing them.
If you'd like to leave a review on Amazon, please do!
Reviews make this indie super happy!

Come & say hi, and to keep up with news on Addie and
Xander here

Facebook Page:
https://www.facebook.com/sloanemurphybooks

Come join my Reader Group for exclusive giveaways &
excerpts!
https://www.facebook.com/groups/sloanes.soldiers/

Twitter & Instagram:
@author_sloanem

Author Note

There have been so many people who have helped me with this series so far, that it is impossible for me to say thank you to everyone individually, because I know what I'll forget someone.

Firstly, thank you to you for continuing with Xander and Addie's journey. I'm sure at this point you have more than a few choice words for me, but I swear, it will all be worth it in the end. I wouldn't be here without you, and without you, there would be no reason for book 3.

To my Alpha's & Betas, thank you for helping me with this at the drop of a hat. It has all been worth it!

To my PA, Danielle Swainson, thank you for putting up with everything, god knows there's enough to put up with! Thank you for keeping my ass in check, and keeping me focused.

To my family, thank you for all of your support, and a big shout out to my mum for having her 'proud mum' moment and shouting about my book from the rooftops.

To Chris, thank you for sacrificing, for allowing me to spread my wings and take this amazing journey.

To Jade, for your stunning covers, I bow down to your genius. Thank you for bringing to life the vision in my head.

Lastly, a big thank you to my editor Katie, for putting up with my crazy PMS'ing during edits. I know I was a royal pain, so again, thank you!

Printed in Great Britain
by Amazon